IT'S JUST A
DOG

A NOVEL BY RUSS RYAN

Thank you for purchasing *It's Just A Dog*. For more information, please visit the book's official website/blog at:

http://www.ItsJustADogBook.com

For questions or comments, please contact the author at this email address:

ItsJustADogBook@gmail.com

A portion of the sales of this book is being donated to the dog-saving superheroes at Muttville Senior Dog Rescue:

http://www.muttville.org

To All The Dogs We've Loved (and Lost) Before...

CONTENTS

IT'S JUST A
DOG

THE DOG STOPS HERE

When I was a boy, we used to visit my grandmother and I would stare mesmerized at an old, framed black-and-white photograph of a family dog that she had hanging above her fireplace. The glum-looking, overweight chocolate Lab had been dead for twenty years, which seemed like an eternity to me back then. I always thought it was kind of creepy, and wondered why my happy-go-lucky grandma still kept this sad, antique doggie pic up on her wall after so much time had gone by.

Now I know why.

My dog just died. Well, it's been six months. But I'm still not over it yet. His name was Pete (not Petey like from *The Little Rascals*—although he was a little rascal) and he was the cutest, crankiest, least affectionate sixteen-and-a-half-year-old Jack Russell terrier that you'd ever want to meet. He was also the love of my life—which, being a straight man on the express train to middle age is not exactly something to brag about. But what can I say? The furry little bastard really rocked my world. Of course, all dog owners think *their* dogs are the most unique, amazing creatures put on this Earth. Unfortunately, I didn't realize how truly special Pete was until *after* he passed away.

Don't worry, I'm not gonna get all *Marley & Me* on you—or pull a *My Dog Skip*. But I can't lie to you either: this losing a dog thing ain't for sissies.

It's embarrassing to admit, but I didn't even cry this much when my dad died—and that's no disrespect because I loved my father dearly. However, with a person, barring unforeseen tragedy, you can at least talk about death and try to come to some sort of peace with it and acceptance or whatever. But with Pete, I can only picture him during that last year, his fuzzy noggin engulfed by that super-sized plastic cone of shame that Pete's vet prescribed due to his deteriorating eyesight and propensity for bumping into things, day and night. Those sweet, sad almond-brown dog eyes, shadowed by hazy cataracts, gazed up at me forlornly, trying to figure out what happened to his once nimble body, puzzled and frustrated at how he couldn't jump up onto the bed anymore, or zip down the stairs, or make it outside without whizzing all over the carpet.

Now I've known plenty of friends who have lost pets and have seen that look of horror when they told me that their beloved dog or cat had been put out to pasture—but nothing can prepare you for that cruel blast of shock and bawl when it's *your* dog. You get so used to seeing them every day that it's doubly devastating when you wake up one morning to discover they're not there.

I tried to brace myself for the end, but the intense

emotions easily sliced through my stubborn male keep-it-inside facade. I had no idea how loud my heart would howl when the finality finally hit that I'd lost my little buddy forever; I didn't expect the strange cries that would suddenly erupt whenever Pete's lovable mug would pop into my head. Pete had toughed it out through so many injuries and illnesses during his senior years—arthritis, gastritis, conjunctivitis and a myriad of other itises—that I thought he might just outlive me. But alas, it was not meant to be.

Losing Pete felt like losing a child—although that's not really fair since I've never even had a kid, let alone lost one. In any event, all I can do is share with you the depth of my own personal painful experience, so please bear with me. Besides, loss is a contest that nobody wants to win.

Even I was surprised by how hard I took Pete's passing. How could I be so foolish and naive? C'mon, toughen up! Don't be such a pussy. You're not the first guy to lose a pet. Dogs live, and then they die. It's part of the deal. That's what everybody knows before you sign the contract to take home your new best friend.

And it's not like I don't have some prior exposure to losing an animal. My childhood dog, Starsky, a playful black poodle-schnauzer mix named after the 1970s TV cop show, *Starsky and Hutch*, bit the dust when I was in fourth grade. (Hutch, his sandy-haired

Lhasa Apso partner in crime, lived down the street.) Coming home one day after school, I found my dad sitting alone at the kitchen table. It was unusual for him to be home so early from work. He broke it to me like a man, "We had to put Starsky down today."

"Down?" I replied obliviously. "Down where?"

"I took him to The Humane Society. They put him to sleep."

"Why, was he tired?" I said, still not getting it.

"No, he was very ill. The doctor said he had a tumor, so that's why he smelled funny. So they euthanized him. He's dead."

"What do you mean dead? You *killed* Starsky, Dad?"

"No, they did. The Humane people. Sorry, kiddo."

I recall feeling pretty shook up by the news and somewhat distrustful of my father's account since Starsky hadn't appeared sick at all to me. But you wouldn't have known it by my reaction then, as I think I just mumbled something, then grabbed a bag of Doritos and scuffled into the other room to go watch the rest of *Scooby Doo*.

Looking back, my lukewarm response to Starsky's demise was not as considerate as I would've hoped, but in my defense, it's a lot different losing a dog as a kid than when you're a grown adult. All those days of getting up early for morning walks, picking up crap, preparing meals, playing with slobbery dog toys, clipping toenails, giving baths, emergency visits to the vet, and picking up more crap before snuggling into bed, and then having to get up and do it all over again. It adds up. It all means something, the responsibility, that another living critter is completely dependent on you for survival.

But let's go back to the beginning. I was living with Liberty, my ironically named performance artist girlfriend, who dumped me out of the blue one day because she yearned for her freedom from me and our slummy one room apartment. She claimed to be too sensitive to break up in person, so she left me a pretentious video message of her reciting some bad poetry, professing how she needed to spread her artistic wings by moving into a 3,000-foot loft space that her parents had bought for her.

Liberty and I had discussed getting a dog together, so to get over her departure, I ventured out to the local pound to find a new roommate. It wasn't as if I needed a puppy to lick my wounds even though, in hindsight, I guess you could call it fate. Walking into the ASPCA that day was like entering a maximum-security prison. There were wild, untamed dogs of all shapes and sizes barking and bouncing off the walls inside their dank, dimly lit cages. *Pick me! Pick me!*

And then I came to the end of the last row and found a dignified little guy just sitting quietly at ease, glaring up at me with a look of contempt: *What took you so long?* This was Pete.

Judging by the condition of Pete's teeth, the ASPCA staffers guesstimated that he was either two or three years old; nobody there could verify his official birthdate. To paraphrase a well-known line from *Casablanca*, of all the dogs in all the dog shelters in all the world. Considering the formidable lineup of available dogs that day at the kennel, one might assume that I saved Pete's life. But the honest-to-God truth is that he saved mine.

Unlike most household pets, I pretty much owe my whole career to that darn dog. I was a starving artist when we first met, and he turned my fading hopes of becoming a professional painter into a full-fledged cottage industry. He was not only my precious pal—he was my meal ticket. Before Pete, I had arrogantly envisioned myself as the next Jackson Pollock or Mark Rothko by painting these humongous abstract paintings with big, bold splashes of color, but quite frankly, nobody gave a shit. So, desperate for cash to pay the rent, I was commissioned by the friend of a friend to do a portrait of their Mack Truck-sized Great Dane. It turned out well evidently, because one thing led to another, and I was soon thrust headfirst into the dog world, deluged with freelance gigs, and became known as Charlie Keefe, Painter of Dogs, aka "The Picasso of Pooch Portraits".

I knew next to nothing about dogs until I started painting them, but thereafter I became a self-taught connoisseur of breeds, quickly discerning the differences between Pit Bulls and Bull Terriers; Cocker Spaniels and Springer Spaniels; Bernese Mountain Dogs and Portuguese Water Dogs; Shih Tzus, Shar-Peis, and Shiba Inus; You get the Pointer—and don't even get me started on the designer hybrid dogs!

Soon enough, my busy schedule forced me to give up my highfalutin modern art designs to exclusively do dog pictures that became so much in demand that I was able to focus my work solely on one dog—Pete—who himself became a minor star on the pet celebrity circuit. (He once even got to sniff the butt of Eddie, his fellow Jack Russell from the popular TV sitcom, *Frasier*, at a Hollywood dog show.)

In fact, you may have seen my commercial work somewhere as Pete's face has been plastered on everything from limited edition prints and posters to calendars, greeting cards, T-shirts, onesies, beer koozies, smartphone cases, and whatever else Donny, my marketing mastermind business partner, could cook up.

Obviously, this isn't high art and hasn't been rewarded with much critical praise as most art pundits are reluctant to jump on the pet portrait bandwagon. For example, one prominent New York critic snarled that my series of *Sunday in the Park with Pete* paintings were "so kitschy and mediocre that Animal Control should unleash a pack of rabid dogs into the gallery to urinate on them," which Pete, being a megalomaniacal marker of his territory, took great offense to.

But a few unkind words never hurt our business—or pleasure. Pete and I shook off the snooty highbrows by doing showings at Petco, Costco, and other major retail outlets. We did live TV talk shows, book signings, and dog charity events (Pete always gave back). This astonishing windfall afforded us a modest home and studio gallery in Carmel-by-the-Sea, California, a quaint coastal village originally founded as an artists colony in the early 1900s, that has since developed into an upscale tourist destination, the home of retired movie stars, C.E.O.'s and Pebble Beach Golf Course, teeming with luxury boutique shops, picturesque cottages, and windswept Cypress trees.

Interviewers used to ask if I ever felt guilty for exploiting my dog for fame and fortune? Hell no! We were a team. We celebrated our victories together, and we commiserated in our defeats. And I always spoiled Pete with the spoils of our success. Pete certainly never complained when he went from a diet of generic kibble and table scraps to USDA Prime Sirloin—and even got miffed when I dared to police his red meat intake.

Having said that, his fluctuating weight hardly affected his popularity. Everywhere we went Pete would get stopped on the street by admiring fans for a hearty pet or belly scratch. *"Where have I seen that dog before?"*

they'd say. *"He looks just like the one from those paintings!"*

Although Pete wasn't the most expressive mutt, he loved being the center of attention—until he got older and I had to cut down his public appearances to only a handful of events a year. Like a fine Cabernet, Pete got better with age, which made it all the more excruciating when he unexpectedly died on me. Just when I had gotten adjusted to life with my boy as a slower, frailer, elderly dog, he mysteriously disappeared.

It is with great regret that I now fully understand why some owners are reluctant to pull the trigger on a sick, older dog. I used to watch these melancholy masters dragging their poor, blind, deaf, crippled companions down the street using contraptions made of straps, harnesses, and wheels and think to myself how cruel, how weak, how selfish these people are for keeping their dogs alive. It's over. Just let them go. Now I get it though. There's a huge difference between your dog being sick and old versus being *dead.* You just want to hang onto your pal as long as you can.

Surely, if my father were here today and heard me going on and on about all this dead dog stuff, he would sit me down and say, "C'mon, it's just a dog, son. It's just a dog."

But this time, he would be wrong. My Pete ~~wasn't~~ isn't just a dog. He's a ghost. And he still haunts me every day.

CHAPTER 1
BON VOYAGE, PETE

The last time I saw Pete alive was right before a big business trip to Paris to attend a retrospective of my dog portraits over the last decade. It was to be the trip of a lifetime, a celebration of my life's work culminating in an international exhibition befit for a king, namely Little Lord Pete.

The only negative was that I could not share the glory with my prince of a pup as Pete was in no condition to endure a twelve-hour plane ride. And he was not happy about it. So, I tried to soften the blow by picking him up for one last dance and sing him a song, my shaky voice echoing off the interior slats of his plastic cone, "*Everytiiiime we say good-byyyyyyye, I die a lit-tle...*"

Little did I know how prophetic those lyrics would be.

"Let's go, Charlie, you're gonna be late!" Donny, my consigliere, waved out at the cab in the driveway to take me to the airport. Donny was a superb businessman, but not much of a dog lover. Yet after selling so many Pete paintings over the years, which easily outsold all of the other artists on his client list combined, he learned to appreciate the palette of Pete.

I kissed Pete on the nose and set him back down

into his favorite position on the couch. He glared back up at me with his guilt trip-laden face that he had so beautifully mastered since adolescence.

"Love ya, little man," I teased him. "No, I love you more. No, I love you more!" I tore off a hunk of sausage from my plate. "Okay, one more for the road?"

Pete morosely turned his head away. He wasn't going to let me off the hook easy this time. I put on a brave face because it was always tough leaving him, even with close friends looking after him.

"All right, you be a good boy for Uncle Donny, okay? I'll bring you back some fancy cheese. Oh yeah, and don't poop in my shoes."

That was Pete's routine manner of expressing his displeasure whenever I left town. One time I came back from a vacation in Miami to discover my front closet looking like it was hit by Hurricane Diarrhea.

"Don't worry, Alissa and I will take good care of Pete," Donny wheeled in the luggage. "We'll make sure the cat doesn't eat him."

Pete grumbled, not even a faint smirk cracked his lips. He was not in the mood for jokes.

"Pete doesn't look right," I turned to Donny. "Does he look okay to you?"

"He's fine," Donny reassured me, taking a big quaff of red wine. "He just wants you to hurry up and leave, so he can go masturbate."

"You're drinking already?" I razzed Donny. "It's not

even noon."

"I'm not an alcoholic—I'm a wine snob. Alcoholics drink anything. I only drink the good stuff."

"If anything happens to him, I'll kill you," I spurned Donny, then returned my attention back to Pete. "Take care, buddy. Be back on Tuesday."

I grabbed my bags and headed out the door, but as I glanced back through the front window, I saw Pete sitting inside staring back at me with a haunting look in his eyes that I just can't get out of my head. He must have known that was the last time we would ever see each other again. Or so I thought.

If you've ever been to Paris in the spring, it is everything they say it is and more. The bigger revelation is why would such a magical city as Paris want anything to do with little old me, Mister Painter of Dogs? After all, this is the place where the art of painting— specifically, Impressionism and Post-Impressionism— was invented. This was the city of Matisse, Monet, and Toulouse-Lautrec. I wasn't remotely within orbit of that world-class league of artists. The only thing we had in common is that we both used oil and brushes.

The truth is, this art show wasn't about me. It was about Pete and the love of dogs. The French are notorious for adoring their pooches even more than Jerry Lewis, taking them along everywhere they go—to the cafes, bookshops, and department stores. Being the ultimate doggie Mecca, perhaps Hemingway was speaking for all canines when he deemed Paris *A Moveable Feast.*

That's another thing about all of us crazy dog owners: no matter where you go, there we are. Up at the crack of dawn, dawdling down crooked sidewalks, trailing our faithful mates at all hours of the night. Standing on street corners waiting for the light to change. Sitting outside coffee shops holding an extra chair. Cutting our way through dark alleyways, the telltale plastic baggie sticking out of our pockets, whether it's a grungy pair of sweats, or the finest couture. The everyday *joie de vivre* one gets from having a dog is universal.

I cannot begin to tell you how surreal it is to see your name on a marquee emblazoned with klieg lights — *GALERIE HUREL PRESENTE L'ART DE CHIENS by CHARLIE KEEFE* — in The City of Light, no less, as my French escort-slash-translator, Genevieve, a petite brunette scholar sporting serious bangs, and I pulled up to the opening night reception party. Sure, it wasn't the Louvre, but it was an unbelievably decadent venue for a dog painter with its centuries-old building, ornamented by gilded crown moldings and sky-high ceilings in the main entrance hall. It was a personal and professional high to see my oeuvre of puppy paintings showcased on such a grand scale. Even Pete would've been impressed.

To my surprise, the studied, sophisticated Genevieve was so excited to meet The Painter of Pete that she peppered me with questions about him and her own wire-haired Jack Russell in broken Frenglish: *"So what is Monsieur Pete really like? Does he have allergies like my Pierre? Is the spot on his eye genuine or did you draw it on him?"*

The lone drawback to being surrounded by such dedicated dog lovers as the French is that nobody else at the party spoke English—or wanted to—as far as I could tell. Schmoozing has never been my forte, let alone schmoozing in another language. The Q&A part of the evening was equally treacherous as I'm not much of a public speaker, preferring to let my work do the talking. In the past, Pete was the perfect icebreaker at these types of events because he usually stole the show by just sitting there cutely without saying a peep.

I stood behind the front podium and took cover as the foreigners' questions came flying at me fast and furiously, slowed momentarily by the transmission delay from Genevieve's skilled translation. A number of audience members had picked up on Pete's absence and seemed more curious about him than my work:

"Où est Pete?" ("Where is Pete?")

"Pourquoi est-Pete pas avec vous?" ("Why is Pete not

with you?")

"Pete est malade?" ("Is Pete not feeling well?")

"Quel est l'age de Pete?" ("How old is Pete?")

"Combien de temps pensez-vous de Pete vont vivre?" ("How long do you think Pete will live?")

"Combien de temps les chiens comme Pete généralement vivre?" ("How long do dogs like Pete live?")

"Mon chien vient de mourir. Vous peindre mon chien?" ("My dog just died. Will you paint my dog?")

"Que ferez-vous peindre quand Pete n'est plus avec nous, ici sur Terre?" ("What will you paint when Pete is no longer with us on Earth?")

"Look, this show is supposed to be about the art—not the life expectancy of my dog," I lashed back at the Frenchies. "So, please. No more questions about Pete."

The room fell silent after Genevieve relayed my testy reply. Realizing I had offended the crowd, which jeopardized my all too consuming need to be liked, my forehead grew flush and shiny with perspiration. But then, a college-aged questioner saved me by grabbing the microphone and speaking up in perfect English, "I understand. I get angry, too, when people call my dog fat."

The auditorium exploded with laughter, and we finished up with no more awkward interludes. Luckily, no one held my prickliness against me, as it possibly may have even alleviated their doubts that I was a legitimate painter since the French prefer their artists rude and combative.

Once the interrogation ended, I scurried off the stage and went on to enjoy the rest of the night with the aid of several high-octane Absinthe cocktails. In spite of that, I still couldn't drown the lingering worries of Pete out of my mind because my worst fears were about to be confirmed.

A few years ago, a former fling had suggested after we split up that the reason I was so obsessed with my dog is because I'd been too deeply hurt in my past experiences with women—so that's why I chose the safe, trusted companionship of a mutt over a dame. I vehemently rejected this pop psychology analysis. I loved women. Loved talking to them, loved being around them. I just had never met one who was as much fun to be with all the time as Pete. He had been my longest relationship by far.

Also, being an artist, I'm a fairly shy, introverted person. And specializing in doggie portraiture, you don't meet too many female groupies—mostly just kind, like-minded fans in shabby, dog hair-encrusted sweaters. So when French Girl, a tall Brigitte Bardot-ish stunner in a plum scoop dress, strutted up with a flute of Veuve Clicquot, I couldn't turn her away—even if I had no clue what she was saying since Geneviève had deserted me for the ladies room. Naturally though, I'd like to think our body language was off the charts.

As our conversation floundered, I couldn't tell if French Girl had mistaken me for someone else, or if she liked my dog paintings on the wall—or even dogs, for that matter. But it wasn't important because I was so thrilled to be talking to a gorgeous woman in one of the most gorgeous cities in the world, as well as not fretting if Pete was back home defecating into my brand new Nikes. To the non-French fluent passerby, here's what our inane dialogue must've sounded like:

FRENCH GIRL: *Bonsoir, Monsieur! ?Á&#*^??*
ME: *Ummm, yeah...Bonjour. Oui, oui!*

Then my cellphone rang. I checked the readout: *DONALD BERGMAN CALLING* (Donny). I pressed IGNORE. Whatever was happening back in California could wait. Nothing was going to ruin my big night in The City of Light. Besides, I was just trying to get into the flow of this nonsensical tête-à-tête before French Girl figured out that I wasn't a real artist.

FRENCH GIRL: *&*?!!%#Á**!*$^!!!*
ME: *Ha, ha! Je ne sais quoi!*

My cell rang again. *DONALD BERGMAN CALLING.* Ignore.

FRENCH GIRL: @*&#*$$%^?!(=%+^$@!..?!?!!
ME: *Yes, yes. C'est la vie!*

Then my phone buzzed a third time: *DONALD BERGMAN CALLING.* What could he want at this hour? This was so unlike Donny to call repeatedly. He preferred texting. I politely excused myself from French Girl and finally answered, "What's up, Donny boy, you drunk? I'm the artist—I'm the one who should have a drinking problem."

"No," Donny's voice answered soberly, "it's about Pete."

"Can I call you later? This place is a zoo, I can barely hear you—"

"Pete's not doing so good."

"What?" I hustled over to a quiet corner past the coatroom. "What do you mean?"

"It started last night," Donny continued. "He was acting listless, didn't touch his dinner. I thought he was still sulking about you leaving, but then when Alissa went to take him out for a walk this morning, she found him lying off his bed, unable to get up, coughing up blood and foam."

"Did you take him to the vet?" I stiffened up in alarm. Pete hated going to the vet even more than me leaving town.

"That's where we are right now."

"So what'd Doctor Paula say?"

There was a long, belabored pause.

"She says his kidneys are failing. Doctor Paula's done several tests, but Pete's not responding well and it's very painful. She thinks it's time to...put him to sleep."

This hit me like a sucker punch, a lethal body shot that buckled my knees.

"Put him to sleep? You mean, like, right *now*? Can't we at least wait 'til I get back?"

"I'm sorry, Charlie. I know how difficult this must be for you, but Doctor Paula says he's in a lot of pain."

"Okay, well, let me think about it. Call you back in ten minutes," I hung up, shell-shocked, as Pete's health crisis brought my world crashing back down to earth. The night had started off like a dream, but was ending in a nightmare.

Then French Girl and her saucy pal ran up to me giggling, and shoved a large poster-sized print of Pete in my face. It was one of my early paintings that I'd done just a week or so after I had first gotten him.

"Excusez-moi, would you sign please?" French Girl gleamed. "Votre chien est très belle!" Translation: your dog is beautiful.

I took one look at Pete's smiling face and broke down.

Later that night, after making the toughest call of

my life, I sat on the edge of the hotel bed and drunkenly gazed out the window at The Eiffel Tower lit up across the Seine like a Christmas tree. It looked so fake. Nothing seemed real anymore. Then my phone beeped with a text from Donny that simply read: *It's done. RIP PETE.*

Just like that, it was over. My best friend in the whole wide world was gone. *Au revoir, Pete.* Like Picasso a century before me, I would now be entering my very own blue period.

CHAPTER 2
IN THE DOGHOUSE

Suffice to say, the plane ride home was not a pleasant one. And it had nothing to do with getting stuck with the middle seat. The only passengers that flight must have seemed longer for were the unlucky fellas trapped on both sides of me who were constantly jolted from their slumbers by my sudden, intermittent sobs of agony. I struggled to hold my feelings inward and embrace the pain, but the pressure kept building and building until I could not contain them. Strange, high-pitched squeaks and wails escaped without warning. I bit my lip and twisted into a pretzel, but the overpowering emotions would not surrender. There were noises coming out from so deep inside me that they didn't even sound like I was the one making them.

Thankfully, after we reached cruising altitude, things calmed down. But then images of that last day with Pete would zoom through my brain to reignite the turbulence and sent me screaming back on a one way trip to despair.

I tried numbing the pain with a steady stream of Jack and Cokes, but alcohol couldn't salve this wound. What made things worse was that it seemed that even the in-flight satellite TV stations had conspired against me as every channel I turned to was airing some program about dogs. CNN featured a heartwarming story of a disabled Iraq war vet and his trusty Rottweiler; Animal Planet had a thing on about rare dog show breeds; *Beverly Hills Chihuahua* was playing on The Disney Channel, and the infamous *Dog Whisperer* was on National Geographic.

Then, at last, I found a dog-less romantic comedy. Unfortunately, this movie turned out to be *Four Weddings and a Funeral,* which has that big tearjerker scene when Hugh Grant's friend eulogizes his gay partner by reading the heartbreaking poem, *Funeral Blues,* by W.H. Auden (*"He was my North, my South, my East and West..."*). After watching that clip, I couldn't help but think of Pete and lost it all over again. Seriously, if you haven't read or heard of the Auden poem before, Google it. You'll cry like a banshee, regardless if your dog has died recently or not.

To kill time on the endless transatlantic flight, I went through the entire Kubler-Ross model of The Five Stages of Grief to try and make sense of Pete's demise. Here are a few notes I scribbled down on a napkin:

1. DENIAL - *Pete's dead? No way! He's just waiting for me at home right now, all cuddled up on the couch.*

2. ANGER - *This is NOT fair. After all I did for that dog and this is how he re-pays me? THAT UNGRATEFUL LITTLE SHIT!*

3. BARGAINING - *Okay, God, let's make a deal. I promise if you bring Pete back alive, I will donate* ~~50%~~ ~~80%~~ *ALL of my future earnings to dog shelters and volunteer at dog rescue groups. For the rest of my life. Cross my heart, hope to die, stick a doggie thermometer in my eye!*

4. DEPRESSION - *What's the frickin' point? Life is meaningless without Pete. Didn't he know that we were supposed to go together? What if I just got up and ripped open the emergency door and jumped out of this plane?*

5. ACCEPTANCE – *Pete's gone. Oh well. He had a great life. Filled with lots of love and walks and treats. Think of all the other dogs out there who lead awful lives and are beaten or neglected or euthanized way before their time...Ugh. WHERE OH WHERE DID MY SWEET BOY GO? COME BACK, PETE, COME BAAACCKKKKKK!!!*

After completing the steps, I re-read what I wrote and slugged my tray table in anguish, jarring the poor guys snoozing next to me. I apologized profusely and looked down at my watch. There were still eight more hours before we were scheduled to land.

"Welcome back," Donny said, picking me up at the airport gate, plunking a gift-wrapped bottle of wine and a small, cheap, wood veneer box into my paunch. "Here, Pete wanted you to have this."

"What is it?"

"It's a 40-year-old tawny port. So *delish*—"

"No, this," I pointed at the box.

"Oh, that's Pete," Donny added. "His ashes."

I took the box and smoothed my fingers over a chintzy metal plate screwed into the side with an engraved inscription that said *PETEY.* This was it? This was all that was left of my one true puppy love? It looked so unfitting a final resting place for such a noble soul as my little, four-legged king. And they spelled his name wrong. It was Pete, *not* Petey.

"What, you cremated him?" I grilled Donny. "I wanted to bury him in the backyard."

"Sorry. I texted you and you never wrote back, so I thought it was cool," Donny answered. "What was I supposed to do? Keep him in the icebox till you got back?"

Donny had a point. I've never been very well organized when it comes to the day-to-day details of life—and the logistics of disposing Pete's remains never made it onto my To-Do List. Donny's response also took me back to a funny story going around the dog park a few months ago about a kooky, eccentric dog bachelor named Lionel who was rumored to have kept his cherished Pomeranian in his freezer for over two years after she died. After hearing the sordid tale, we all laughed about it and thought the guy was a nut job, but now having gone through my own doggie tragedy, I have to admit the idea no longer sounded completely bonkers. It might be a reasonable alternative for keeping your old dog around, if you could handle the messiness of taxidermy involved. Pardon the gallows humor, but Pete and I always had a thing for dark comedy.

During the last year, when Pete's decline was becoming more evident and impossible to ignore, I used to joke with him on our walks at his favorite park about potential spots where he might like to be laid to rest. *How 'bout the back entrance with a view overlooking the pond? Perhaps the wide-open field behind the playground would be more your style? Or what about under the softball diamond bleachers where you love digging for gophers?*

At the time, it seemed like a healthy, lighthearted way to deal with Pete's bleak future. But now that he was actually dead and gone, it wasn't very amusing at all.

Finally, when I got back home, words cannot describe how quiet the house was. The silence. There is no quieter place than the home of a dog owner the day after his or her prized pooch has passed. It was like a cleaning service had come in while I was away and sucked the life out of the place. Everything appeared the same and in its rightful place—the furniture in the living room, the pictures on the walls, the tchotchkes in the display cabinet—but the most important thing of all was missing: Pete. And it left a huge, gaping hole not only in my heart, but in the house as well.

I've heard other dog owners talk about dog energy, but I always thought it was a bunch of spiritual mumbo-jumbo conjured up by dog fanatic extremists. Not anymore. The absence of Pete was palpable. His spirit had left the building. The only good part was that I didn't find any crap in my shoes, although part of me even missed that traditional homecoming present.

I set down Pete—or, what was left of him in the shoddy wood box—and there I saw it: his old dog collar and plastic cone sitting lifelessly on the kitchen counter where Donny had left them after returning from the vet's on that last fateful day.

I picked up the collar and gently held it in my hands, the bone-shaped dog tag marked *Pete* jangling in my hands, the way it had jangled so many times before on our daily adventures. Only this time, there was no doggie inside to make it sing. Inexplicably, I then attempted to put the collar on and, amazingly, it fit even though my neck had to be twice the size of Pete's. But then suddenly, I felt a surge of adrenaline, and the collar tightened firmly around my jugular with a mind of its own—a life force, if you will. My heart raced faster, and I began to hyperventilate. Then I heard what sounded uncannily like Pete's footsteps tip-tapping in from the other room behind me, as if busting me in the middle of a late night snack, as he had done so many times before. I quickly spun around, expecting to see him standing in the doorway—but nobody was there. Just a tree branch banging against the window shutters outside.

Spooked, I snapped the collar off and tossed it into a drawer, then sadly trudged off to bed, dog-tired.

CHAPTER 3
LIFE AFTER DOG

Alfred Lord Tennyson, the 19th Century poet, famously once wrote that it's better to have loved and lost than not to have loved at all—but I bet he never had a dog. With all due respect to Starsky, losing my boyhood pup was child's play compared to this. The days and weeks ahead were spent in a fog as the harsh reality of no more Pete sank in. It was hard to even fathom what my life was like before Pete. For the last thirteen-plus years, my body clock trained me to automatically pop up at 7 a.m. and head out the door for our morning walk, but now there was nowhere to go.

I couldn't go into any room without constantly being reminded of Pete at every turn, whether it was passing by his old leash hanging on a doorknob, or tripping over a chewed-up toy, or just being stared at by his many portraits adorning the walls. Every cupboard I opened was jam-packed with used doggie supplies. What with all the dog brushes, tools, and meds that Pete had stockpiled during his life span, I could open a pet store. This dead dog had more stuff than I did!

Yes, my boy had left his mark on every square foot of our living space, both literally and figuratively. No spot had been untouched by his mangy little paws or relentless shedding of dog hair. By the way, can anybody tell me how does dog hair get into the refrigerator or stuck to the top of the ceiling? It's a mystery. I predict that when Earth is destroyed a billion years from now in a fiery explosion, there will still be traces of dog hair lying around to let future life know of our existence. Remember, you heard it here first.

When I felt okay enough to go out in public, I drove over to my mom's house in Watsonville to help her with some chores, but that only caused further unrest. After all, this woman had been an accomplice in Starsky's "execution" at the hands of my father many moons ago without a word of remorse.

"That's a shame about Pete," she tried to sympathize. "So sad." And then in the same breath, she said, "Look what I got at the store today. Candied walnuts. On sale!"

I wanted to grab her by her dainty shoulders and scream, *Mom, how can you talk about walnuts at a time like this? Pete's not just a dog—he's my boy. My boy is dead!"*

"Look on the bright side," Mom went on. "You think you have it rough? I had three friends die last year."

"Mom, this isn't a competition," I sighed.

Donny put on a nice memorial gathering for Pete at the art gallery, a.k.a. The House That Pete Built, as all of his old pals from the neighborhood showed up to pay their respects. I knew most of the dogs' names, but not their owners—other than my personal nicknames for them such as The Redhead With The Two Vizslas, or Walter the Weimaraner's Dad—as we feasted on some of Pete's favorite chow of pizza squares, sausage links, and lamb lung treats.

At the party, everyone was incredibly supportive, albeit a tad distant, as if I was contagious with a fatal disease and any contact with me could somehow infect *their* dog. I understood their reticence. Like most well-meaning folks, they probably just didn't know what to say.

Another thing that got my dander up was when Greg and Marina, a likable young couple, asked if I was going to get a new dog. The thought of replacing my loyal, old dog with a new model like he was a sports car just seemed disrespectful. It felt like I'd be cheating on Pete. Trying to go out and replace Pete with another dog right away was as silly to me as trying to replace my parents with a couple gray-haired strangers that I just met on the street. I loved Pete with all my heart and soul—and to rush out and get another dog to fill his collar, just so I wouldn't have to continue suffering, didn't feel kosher. And it wouldn't be fair to the new dog either. The only dog I wanted was the one dog that I could never, ever have again.

Several more friends called and sent cards to offer

condolences. Donny's wife, Alissa, even penned a touching obit on Pete's Facebook and Twitter pages, which rapidly filled up with warmhearted messages:

OMG...So sorry for your loss:(

<3<3<3 God Bless Pete <3<3<3

Don't cry because it's over...Smile because it happened.

Pete's up in doggie heaven running with the big dogz!

And then there was always the occasional troll:

DOGHATER WROTE: *Boo F***ING hoo. Dogs suck. CATS RULE!!!!*

I know what you're thinking: a dead dog with a Twitter account? What's this world coming to? All I can tell you is that 179,448 followers can't be wrong, can they? The digital outpouring was overwhelming, but what I needed right now was a hug, not a thousand compassionate comments.

As kind and hopeful as these well-wishers were, I was having a tough time coming to terms with the concept of an afterlife. Some fellow dog widowers tried to boost my spirits with tales of The Rainbow Bridge, a mythological wonderland where all pet owners will supposedly be reunited with their deceased pets in the next world. But I just couldn't quite wrap my head around the idea of a heavenly kingdom for dogs—or any animals. I mean, yes, I grew up going to Sunday school and church and, even if I wasn't that religious as an adult, I still believed in heaven and hell for humans. For some reason though, a doggie Eden with pearly gates just didn't seem quite as plausible. And the whole dog-spelled-backwards-is-God mantra, while vaguely comforting, failed to provide much solace.

In short, I had a long list of questions, but no answers. Was Pete really in a better place? Would I ever see him again? I genuinely wanted to believe in the possibility, but my faith was wavering. What was the point of all our accomplishments and good times together if we just turn to dust in the end?

And the hardest part to swallow—the part that kept gnawing away at me like Pete used to gnaw on a juicy marrowbone—was that I couldn't forgive myself for not being there when he was put to sleep. Even though I felt justified pulling the plug, there was still tremendous guilt. No matter how much love and affection (and credit card bills) I had lavished on Pete, I still couldn't get over the fact that I was not there for him during his darkest hour. I just couldn't erase what I pictured to be Pete's utter sense of terror and abandonment when the vet stuck the needle in and he looked up for his proud master, but I was nowhere in sight. Taking into account all he had done for me and my career, it seemed unforgivable. The Grim Dog Reaper had come calling, and I wasn't there to hold him one last time and bid him adieu because I was too busy living the high life off his good name. And now there was hell to pay.

On top of losing my muse, I also lost my mojo. I couldn't work. Had no desire to paint or draw. Even getting out of bed was a chore. In the mornings, I'd shuffle into my studio and stare at a blank canvas trying to dream up new creations, but there were no sparks of inspiration. I just sat at my computer and burned through most afternoons watching cutesy pet videos on YouTube, which made me miss Pete even more, or making iPhoto slideshows of my dearly departed dog, alternating soundtracks between sentimental Sarah McLachlan (*"I Will Remember You"*), mournful Eric Clapton (*"Tears In Heaven"*) and bittersweet Cat Stevens (*"I Love My Dog"*), for whatever funk I was in. Admittedly, these weren't the most original choices of slideshow music, but they were remarkably cathartic in airing out some of my grief.

Donny, growing concerned with my inability to move on, wanted Alissa to set me up with her single friends to keep me occupied.

"Just go out and have fun," Donny pep talked me. "There's a ton of women in this town looking for a nice, successful guy like you. It'll be like shooting monkeys in a barrel."

"I think you're mixing animal metaphors," I countered. "It's fish in a barrel. Shooting a barrel full of monkeys sounds pretty sick and disturbing."

"Whatever, you know what I'm saying," he reiterated. "You've been so consumed with Pete that you haven't been with anyone in a long time. Do it for Pete. He'd want you to get laid."

"No, he wouldn't," I disagreed, recounting how Pete used to jump up on the bed whenever I had female guests over, nuzzling his way between me and any shot at foreplay. "That greedy cock-blocker sabotaged my sex life."

Donny switched course and tried setting me up with a new dog, bombarding me with texts and emails with attached mug shots of huggable hounds up for adoption. After lunch on slow days, we stood outside the gallery ogling the parade of tourists and their pet pups strolling by—a who's who of perky Puggles, dapper Dachshunds, and incorrigible Corgis. Despite their cuteness, they might as well have been from another planet because they all seemed like aliens to me.

"What about that one?" Donny would say, pointing out his picks of the litter. "He's a funny character. Or that guy? Lookit that face!"

After I snubbed several of these fne puppies without showing a smidgen of interest, he finally threw in the towel. "Why not? What's your problem?"

"That's not my dog," was all I could respond. None of them were Pete. And I just wasn't ready yet.

Sometime before Pete died, my dog park pal, Milo, a charismatic, young, good-looking dog walker dude, gave me his theory on pet loss one night at a Friday night yappy hour (the dog park's version of happy hour where everyone brings refreshments while chaperoning their frolicking pets). After losing numerous clients on the job, Milo theorized that there were two kinds of dog widowers—those who go out and get a new dog right away to take the place of their old one; and those who never get another dog again and grieve for their old dog for the rest of their lives. This made a lot of sense, but it was still too early to tell which camp I was in.

CHAPTER 4

DOG DAYS OF SUMMER

After mooching off Pete's pretty face all these years, I was now forced to find my own way. And I began questioning my talent. There is a certain unexplainable magic to making art. Some days you never really know where it comes from. And now with my favorite subject extinct, I felt like I was being exposed for the true con artist that I really was: a hack, a charlatan, a fraud! Maybe it really was Pete guiding my hand across the canvas all this time, telling me what lines to draw, which colors to use, which shadows to highlight. What kind of dog painter could I be without my dog?

Imagine back in the day if Cezanne was forbidden to paint fruit, or if Warhol was prohibited from silk-screening Campbell's Soup cans? That's how I felt in the studio without Pete lying at my feet on the floor, slowly rotating his position throughout the day to follow the patch of sunlight peeking in through the skylights, the bright rays of sunshine serving as his own personal spotlight, as he was the real star in the family.

Nevertheless, Donny didn't have time to reflect on the guiding light of our enterprise. We had a business to run, and the numbers guy was losing patience. With no new paintings coming in and old bills piling up, his last email sounded more like marching orders than a courtesy call:

> **From:** DBergman
> **Subject:** What's up?
> **To:** CharKeefe
>
> ---
>
> Charlie,
> We need to talk. You don't answer the phone or return my messages. In case you've forgotten, we are not just friends. We are PARTNERS.
>
> You haven't delivered a new painting since April. It's time to get back to work, don't you agree? I know you really miss Pete. We all do. But we need to sell some new work soon or we'll both be out of business.
>
> Call if you need me,
> D.

I clicked the screen off. After that missive from Donny, I needed some fresh air. So I decided to go take a walk, which turned out to be the best idea I had come up with in a long time.

You'd be amazed to learn how many people you meet when you're out walking a dog. As someone who spent most of his day stuck inside an art studio breathing in paint fumes, it was vitally important to get outside every so often for some perspective. All those years of taking Pete out for his daily stroll, I always thought I was doing it for him, but in fact, he did it for me.

Since Pete was gone, these jaunts around town past all of our old haunts were non-existent. Walking by the local dog park now was like walking past a cemetery. What once used to be such a joyous oasis for my boy and me was a stark reminder of everything that was missing in my life.

Now I'm sure all of my old dog park buds would've gladly welcomed me back with open arms, it just didn't feel the same to go in there without Pete. And stopping to observe the clusters of happy pooches and their beaming owners only made it worse, as bitter, resentful thoughts darkened my mind. How come all *their* dogs—that Pete used to run around and play with for years—are alive and kicking on this glorious day while mine was reduced to a pile of rubble? I wanted to shake these duped dog owners from their giddy states of bliss and forewarn them, *"You know they die, right? They really do die!"*

In a way, I felt sorry for these lucky dogs. They had no idea what kind of torture was waiting for them. Even the most sensible first-time dog owners can't help but live in denial, secretly believing that death only happens to other people's dogs.

Two dog walkers standing at the far end of the run recognized me loitering by the fence and waved me in to come join them. But I wasn't up for small talk, so I just gave them a friendly salute and hurried along on my way.

"Pete!" I then heard someone bark behind me. *"PEEEEETE!"*

I turned around to see a frazzled woman jogging toward me with a pack of off-leash dogs. This was Janice, or Jeanette, who I had met several times before at the dog park. She was a scattered, but nice enough person—a short, strong-willed thirty-something natural beauty who rarely wore makeup—a fetching Fox Terrier in blue jeans. I don't think we'd ever had a full conversation before because she was always trying to pawn off one of her shelter dogs to anyone within earshot, as she was a fervent dog rescue volunteer who had made it her life's mission—and everyone else's—to find homes for all of her scruffy clients. Her heart was in the right place, but she did sometimes come off as pushy and a bit of a ball-buster, which was ironic since a good portion of her non-profit group's funds was spent on neutering stray males.

"Hi, I thought that was you," she caught up to me, out of breath. "You're the guy with the Jack Russell, right?"

"I'm Charlie," I answered. "Pete was my dog's name."

"Omigosh, sorry. That's me. Janelle the Absent-Minded Dog Lover. I always remember the dog's name, never the owner's."

I nodded cordially, recalling her name, but not liking where this was headed. Could we please talk about something other than dogs, please?

"So where's Pete?" Janelle wanted to know.

"Haven't seen you guys at the park in a while."

I paused, uneasy. It was at times like this that I needed to suck it up and gather my strength to share the sad news. However, this was not one of those times.

"Pete's doing great," I lied. "Back at the house. Sleeping off his hangover. Too many margaritas last night."

"You gave your dog tequila?" Janelle eyed me with scorn.

"No, that was a joke," I fumbled. "Just some drunken doggie humor for you."

"Ohhhh," she blanched awkwardly.

"Okay, well, good seeing you," I took a step, moving along.

"Listen, before you go," Janelle stopped me. "I wanted to invite you and Pete to my charity event that we're having out at the farm," she said, foisting a color-copied flyer into my hands:

FOSTER DOG FUN FAIR
Saturday, 11 AM - 4 PM
Brought to you by your friends @ Foster Dogs Forever
"Save A Life, Foster A Dog"
JANELLE JORDAN, CEO/Owner

"It's going to be a blast. We're having a raffle, a pet costume contest, and prizes galore. So we would love to see you two there. Oh, and if you want to donate one of your dog paintings to help the cause—"

"Thanks, but we can't make it," I cut her off hastily.

"Why not?"

"Because. Pete's *dead*."

"What?" Janelle looked upset.

"Yeah, I should've said something before, but it's been a really tough time. And it's hard to talk about so..."

"Don't be sorry. I know what it's like to lose a dog," she empathized, leaning in to give me a long, heartfelt embrace. "It's. The. Worst."

"Tell me about it. I can't believe it still hurts this bad. I mean, I'm a grown man and Pete was just a dog."

"No, he wasn't just a dog. He was *your* dog. And it's nothing to be embarrassed about. I think it's beautiful you loved him so much," she impressed upon me. "How long's it been?"

"Three months," I exhaled, feeling the tears well up. I tried not to break, but there was something in her eyes that brought it pouring out of me, another shameful public display of affliction.

"It's okay," Janelle squeezed me tighter. "You did the right thing."

"No, I didn't do anything," I confessed. "I wasn't even there with him when he died. I was out of town. For work."

"I'm sure Pete understands. You may not be able to hold him in your arms, but you'll always hold him in your heart."

This nutty dog chick might have been full of

clichés, but she was making me feel better. Until she blurted out, "So when are you getting a new one?"

"What?" I asked, hoping I'd heard her wrong.

"Don't let this crush you. I cried for a year after my heart dog, Topper, died. And you know what? The day I stopped crying is the day I got a new dog. I know it might seem too soon, but you have to keep your heart open or it'll close up forever."

Now them were fighting words. Just because my heart was broken didn't mean it was defective.

"What's that supposed to mean?" I snapped.

"Sorry, I don't mean to push. We all have our own timelines for grieving—and Pete could never be replaced. But we do have some great dogs out at the farm that would be perfect for you."

"No thanks, I don't need another dog. I'm still trying to get over my last one."

"Then maybe you should think about fostering. It's very healing. You don't have to keep the dog permanently. You just foster it until we find their forever home."

I trembled, my blood beginning to boil. To me, personally, fostering dogs was for suckers. It seemed like a passive-aggressive way for these dog-saving superheroes to manipulate you into taking in one of their undesirable mutts. They knew full well that if you had even half a heart, then you would fall totally, helplessly in love with the troublemaking little scalawag and be stuck with it for good.

"So what do you think?" Janelle pressed on. "Can we put your name on the list as a future foster parent?"

Now at this point is where a gracious, well-mannered gentleman would just keep his mouth shut and weasel out of the request without making any guarantees. Sad to say, this wasn't me.

"Have you listened to a word I said? My dog's *DEAD!*" I blew up at her. "Why would I want another dog? So I could have my heart ripped out and chewed up again in a few years? No thanks. I'd rather be alone than go through that twice!"

Janelle stepped back, stunned, as the normal dogged look of determination on her face was now a combination of fright and bewilderment.

"Fine, I can see that I touched a nerve. Just trying to help. Let's go, guys," she calmly tugged her dogs and abruptly fled, leaving me standing there alone to stew in my angry bile.

A few dog park regulars glared across the street at me, cautiously reaching for their cellphones in case things escalated. Even the dogs looked unsettled by my little tirade. Now I was the one who felt like a creep.

"Uh, hey, I'm sorry..." I meekly called out after Janelle. "I'm just not ready for another dog yet!"

She didn't bother breaking stride to hear my mea culpa and disappeared around the bend. Having made a huge ass of myself, I sheepishly turned and head-downed it back the other way to my studio, under the disapproving glares of the remaining dog park dogs and their keepers.

CHAPTER 5
RESCUE ME

Carmel is a small, sleepy town. So when there's a riff between two of its more high-profile residents, people will talk. After a public spat like that, you expect to read about it in our local weekly paper, *The Pine Cone*. I hadn't been out and about since my meltdown, but I can only imagine what they were saying at the dog park, a place where gossip flies faster than Greyhounds around a racetrack.

Donny was dismayed by the bad publicity since he had already heard various versions of the dust-up from our neighboring main street merchants. By the time the story made it down to Ocean Avenue, I was reportedly raving like a lunatic (no argument there), and waving a gun, threatening to bust some caps in Janelle's dogs. Evidently, my reputation had taken such a hit that some area dog owners were now dubbing me *Cujo*.

"You must apologize," Donny instructed me over the phone.

"For what?"

"For being a jerk. You don't go around yelling at women, threatening to kill their dogs."

"I didn't threaten to kill anybody's dog! I just told her I didn't want to *foster* any of her dogs," I clarified.

"That's not what I heard."

"What did you hear?"

"Doesn't matter," he rationalized. "You were rude and offensive to a woman who happens to be very influential in the local dog community—our core customer base. I already called the city dog commission to try and smooth things over. So you have to apologize."

"But you weren't even there."

"I don't care. Apologize."

I picked up Janelle's flyer on the counter. *Save A Life, Foster A Dog.* Yeah, right. Pete would've gotten a big laugh out of that one.

"Okay, I'll give her a call later," I said.

"No. In person. She's having a big doggie jamboree this afternoon, so get your butt out there and put this thing behind us once and for all."

I hung up begrudgingly. He was right. It was time to man up and go make peace.

When I pulled up to Janelle's pet rescue farm, it was a veritable *Field of Dreams* for dogs. Instead of being surrounded by rows of cornfields, there were dogs as far as the eye could see. This foster dog event looked less like a charity gala and more of a canine carnival with dog-themed rides, obstacle courses, grooming kiosks, and a doggie pool for all the hairy beasts to cool off on this hot, sweltering day. If there is such a thing as dog heaven, this was the closest place to it on Earth.

Still, this didn't make it any easier as I got out of the car and felt the cold stares from the dog park gawkers. This rendezvous was going to be much harder than I thought.

I grabbed a package from the trunk, and I took the long walk up to the farmhouse through a swarm of hounds. It was soothing to be enveloped by so many dogs. I could've sworn I felt Pete walking right there beside me as we made our way up to the big party tent, and spotted Janelle sitting at the front reception table greeting guests. Another foster dog do-gooder nudged her, and she looked up at me disconcertedly, unsure whether to call security or run for the hills.

"Hi, Janelle," I hesitantly approached, tail between my legs. "I'm, uh, really sorry about—"

"Gertie, you need help back there?" Janelle ignored my plea, turning to her colleague.

Gertie shook her head, no.

"I'll help anyway because I don't deal well with crackpots," Janelle walked away, dissing me.

"Hey, come on. Can we call a truce?" I reached out to stop her.

"Don't touch me," she blared, drawing several onlookers. "Hercules, sic 'em!"

Out of nowhere, Hercules, a raggedy Chow mix wearing a clown outfit, came prowling at me, baring a mouthful of jagged teeth.

"What—are you crazy?" I squawked, quaking in my

boots.

"Hmm, that's funny, I thought you were the crazy one after biting my head off at the dog park," she reasoned, as Hercules lunged to take a chunk out of my thigh.

"Hey!" I retreated, as Hercules backed me into the corner. "Look, I'm sorry about freaking out on you the other day. That was not cool. Guess I've been such a wreck about Pete that, um, I don't know—I shouldn't have taken it out on you. Please, just call your dog off, okay?"

"Oh, please. Hercules wouldn't hurt a flea," Janelle glanced back at me expressionless, leaving me hanging for a few more uncomfortable seconds. "The worst he could do is maybe knock you out with his halitosis."

Upon hearing that, Hercules promptly collapsed down onto his side to lick his crotch.

"Fine, apology accepted. But I'm doing this for Pete, not *you*," Janelle made clear, then pointed at the framed canvas in my hands. "What's that?"

"Oh, this?" I untied the package. "Well, to show you I mean business, I brought you this last painting I did of Pete. To raffle off for the dogs. If you want."

I handed her the painting, which I'd finished shortly before my trip to Paris, of Pete standing by his doghouse as the midday sun glistened off his shiny plastic cone like a golden halo.

"*Awww*, what a little angel," she took it and

smiled. "It's beautiful. Are you sure you want to give it up?"

"Yeah, Pete would've wanted it that way," I gushed. Frankly, I wasn't sure what Pete's wishes were, but I needed all the help I could get.

"While you're in such a good mood, have you changed your mind about becoming a foster?" Janelle inquired, picking up a cuddly, brown-and-white King Charles Cavalier out of an enclosure, and shoving her into my arms. "Brownie here would love to have you."

Seriously? Was she joking? Damn, this woman drove a hard bargain.

"We got her in from Sacramento last month. She was on death row," Janelle went in for the kill, as a chorus of solicitous moans inflated the tent. "But now her foster family's going away on a long vacation. And if we don't find a place for her soon, we might have to send her back."

"Umm, well, I'd take her," I dilly-dallied, thinking of an excuse. "But I'm not good with puppies."

"She's not a puppy. She's almost two years old. And potty-trained."

"So then what's wrong with her?" I asked, causing a minor stir. While benevolent and altruistic by trade, some overcrowded dog shelters are forced to exaggerate the facts in order to move more pets through the system since there are just too many to go around. For instance, hyperactive, aggressive dogs are re-branded as 'high energy, loves to play'; high maintenance dogs with complicated health issues 'just need a little TLC'; and dogs who don't get along with other dogs, cats, small children, and just about any other living thing 'could use a few training classes'.

"There's absolutely nothing wrong with Brownie," Janelle quickly refuted. "Poor thing was found in a dumpster. All filthy, malnourished. But we've cleaned her up, gave her all her shots, and now she's ready to rock."

Great, I squirmed. There was no telling where this dog with a sketchy past came from. Did her previous owner ditch her and leave her for dead? Or was she some bug-infested, puppy-faced serial killer on the loose? Although judging by her snugly demeanor, she appeared about as dangerous as a Pixar mouse.

"Okay, this might sound superficial, but I'm not really a big fan of King Charles Cavaliers. They're kind of girly dogs, aren't they?" I waffled, to the disdainful gasps of die-hard dog lovers standing around us. "What, does that make me a bad person?"

"We're just busting your chops," Janelle teased. "Remember, as a foster parent, it's temporary. You don't have to keep her. Just hang onto her a couple weeks until we find her something permanent. It's all the love with only half the responsibility."

I looked into Brownie's honeyed eyes, and she gleefully licked my face. I had to admit, she was a cute little ragamuffin. And she had the softest, silkiest coat, quite unlike Pete's wiry Brillo Pad of a body. But that still wasn't enough for me to commit.

"I'm really sorry," I backpedaled. "I really respect and applaud what your group's doing for these dogs, but I just...I can't."

I handed Brownie back to Janelle and solemnly walked away, feeling terrible about breaking the poor dog's heart. But then when I got to my car, there was a motley crew of Janelle's mutts waiting for me, standing shoulder to shoulder in front of the driver's side door, strongly encouraging me to reconsider.

"I swear, I didn't train them to do that," Janelle and Brownie rolled up behind me, her last chance sales pitch. "They must really like you."

"So if Brownie and I don't get along, I can return her anytime, right?" I proposed, folding under the peer pressure. "No questions asked?"

Janelle smirked gamely, knowing she had me right where she wanted me. "*Yessir*, we have an excellent return policy. And we also do exchanges."

What the hell, I thought. It's temporary.

"Okay, I'll give it a shot," I finally relented.

"Congratulations, you're a new dad!" Janelle exclaimed, ringing her dog bell, and the crowd broke into cheers. I went along with the festive jubilation, but inside I was terrified, as this satiny little stranger wriggled in my arms.

Was this really happening? I cringed to myself. I came here today with only the best of intentions, and now I was leaving with a dog. What a pushover I was. What in ~~God's~~ dog's name had I gotten myself into?

CHAPTER 6
REBOUND DOG

I wish I could tell you that I brought Brownie home and we instantly fell madly in love and lived happily ever after, but life with a new dog is not so simple. There's a learning curve involved. Having been around Pete for so many years, I considered myself an expert on dogs. But it didn't take long to realize that my expertise was strictly limited to the idiosyncrasies of my old dog—which was of little to no use in raising this new girl with all of her quirky, unfamiliar traits. I was now a dog rookie, starting all over again from scratch.

The first night, Brownie woke me up at four in the morning by trampling across my drowsy head. She was panting feverishly and pacing atop the pillows, having what appeared to be a full-blown panic attack. If only she could talk, she might've told me what was giving her the heebie-jeebies.

"What's wrong, girl?" I asked. "You sick? Your tummy ache?"

I rolled out of bed to take her out and slid into my Nikes—and felt a soft, chilly, sludgy sensation. Befuddled, I kicked the shoe off and saw my toes were slathered in shit. Sticky, gooey, ice-cold dog shit. This used to be one of Pete's stupid, old pet tricks, but so unlike Brownie.

"Brownie, did you do that? Bad girl. Bad!"

She put her tail down, mortified, and scampered to the front door, scraping at it with her claws, urgently wanting to go out. Now.

"What's gotten into you?" I gave her the third degree. "Why are you in such a hurry? You already pooed in my shoe."

Being out of dog walking practice, I forgot to leash her, so when I opened the door, she bolted off like a shot into the cool, foggy morning as if escaping from a haunted house. I raced after her down the street, but lost sight of her in the cloudy grey mist. By the time I caught up to her at the end of the block watering the neighbor's bushes, I spotted a coyote lurking on the hillside above, scoping us out. There had been recent sightings in the area, to the great fear of small dog owners, but when I got closer, I realized that it wasn't a coyote at all—it was Pete! I froze in my tracks. This miraculous vision of my dear old dog, sitting proudly in a statuesque pose, with his wavy avalanche of white fur and black spot above his right eye, was unmistakable. I trotted toward him for a closer inspection, but then another marine layer rolled in, and he swiftly evaporated.

No way, I thought, wiping the crust from my eyes. Must be seeing things. Unless Pete was trying to contact me from the dead. Was this a sign? Knowing Pete, he'd be spinning in his grave if he found out another dog was living in *his* house. Chalking it off to a bad night's sleep, I scooped up Brownie and we went back to bed.

The first few weeks of cohabiting with a new dog are mostly spent comparing and contrasting it with your old dog. And the biggest hitch with Brownie was that she was not Pete. But this wasn't necessarily a bad thing—in fact, quite the opposite—as I never realized what a surly, stoic, pain-in-the-butt Pete could be sometimes until I experienced everyday life with such a good-natured, affectionate, little licker as Brownie. If this dog had indeed come from a troubled home, she certainly didn't act like it with her bubbly personality and vivacious spirit.

These two dogs couldn't have been more distinct. Whereas Pete could be grumpy and aloof, Brownie had a cheerful disposition and was extremely attentive, tailing me room to room as if I was The Most Interesting Man In The World. This didn't allow me to get much work done though as it's hard to paint with one hand when you have a dog stuck to the other. Not that I've ever been the most prolific artist anyway.

More discrepancies soon became clear. Pete was a loner who didn't much care to socialize with other dogs; Brownie, however, was your classic *dog whore* who would jump up on any dog or person that gave her the slightest bit of attention. Pete never wanted to sleep in my bed, but Brownie insisted upon spooning next to me, my own personal electric blanket. Pete was a finicky eater who rarely ate the same meal twice in a week; Brownie, on the other hand, was a garbage disposal, scarfing down anything I put down in front of her. Pete was smart, knowing intuitively when I was leaving the house or coming home any time of day, while Brownie was a sweet-hearted ditz who just lived in the present, invariably dazzled by each waking breath. And as far as urinating habits, Pete would take an hour to relieve himself since he needed to spread his scent in fifty different locations while Brownie, being a female, barely went two steps out the door before she squatted and emptied out her entire bladder. Now I'm not saying all of these disparities made Brownie a better dog, but she was definitely an *easier* dog.

Even Mom picked up on these notable upgrades after spending only three minutes with her newest grandchild on Skype. "Oooh, she's a keeper. I like this dog much better," she raved.

"Yeah, just like you always favored Dave over me," I poked fun at her preferential treatment of my little brother who, with his loving wife, had already supplied her with a trio of delightful grandkids.

The other benefit with having Brownie around was also getting to know Janelle. Once you got past her rough edges, she was much funnier and more thoughtful than I imagined her to be since joining her outfit as a foster dad. She would call and drop by periodically to check on Brownie, or we'd meet up at shopping malls and street fairs to mingle with prospective suitors. She worked the room like a politician running for office, sizing up guardians, sussing out the most ideal homes for her dogs. After a few of these pet adoption events though, I grew so attached to Brownie that I started fibbing to Janelle about leaving town for business, to limit Brownie's availability. After missing two weekends in a row, I could tell that she was on to me from the sarcasm in her voice.

"Are you sure you don't want to just keep Brownie for yourself?" she asked. "We can make that happen. Better act now before someone else swoops in and steals her away."

"Don't start. I already fell for your cheesy used car salesman tactics once," I replied.

In truth, the offer was tempting, but I couldn't quite pull the trigger yet. Why buy the dog when you can get all the fun for free? Besides, her hands were full with plenty of other adoptees.

In the evenings, Janelle, Brownie, and I went for nightly walks, just the three of us—or six or eight or thirteen—counting how many fosters Janelle was shuttling around that day. As we trailed our shaggy misfits down the coastline, I tried to comprehend how she got hooked up in the dog salvage biz. Who was this woman? Was she a saint or just plain wacko? I've heard of the stereotypical crazy cat lady, but an unmarried belle with a barnyard full of unwanted dogs? How could anyone taking care of that many mutts *not* be crazy? My gut feeling told me there was no chance that such an intelligent, attractive girl like her could still be on the market unless she had a screw loose.

I asked around at the dog park, but nobody really knew anything personal about Janelle other than that she just truly, sincerely loved dogs. The running joke was that maybe she was the heiress to the Alpo dog food fortune to be able to provide that much grub and shelter for so many pooches. Milo presumed that she was probably a lesbian since the majority of dog rescues he worked with were chock full of gay chicks. His words, not mine.

So, one night while Janelle and I were coming back from the beach with our mates, it just slipped out: "Why aren't you married?"

"I was once," she answered without missing a beat. "For seven months. But then he turned out be a real dog."

"He cheated on you?" I asked.

"No, he *died* on me."

I stopped, taken aback.

"He was forty, I was twenty-three," she continued. "After we moved in together, Kevin forgot to tell me that he had Stage IV lymphoma. Not that it would've changed anything, but it brought up other issues. His doctor told me about the cancer after Kevin passed out during our honeymoon. I think we spent more time at the hospital during our marriage than at home."

"How awful."

"No, we had a lot of good days, too. I was just way too young and immature to deal with it. The one thing that saved me from turning into a total wreck was my Pug, Louie," she remembered fondly. "And then he got hit by a car two weeks after Kevin died."

"Wow, that's the worst story I've ever heard in my life," I said.

"Don't tell anyone," she confided, "but losing Louie felt worse than my husband. Just the unexpected shock of it all."

"And I thought I had it bad with Pete."

"It wasn't easy, but I got over it. Look at all these guys I have now," she said, admiring her harem of foster dogs digging in the sand. "It led me to them."

All this dog karma stuff reminded me of an episode I'd seen on *The Dog Whisperer*. Even though I was skeptical of Cesar Millan's self-promotional, show biz ways, he once said that you don't always get the dog you want, but the dog that you *need*. So far, in my case, truer words have never been spoken.

I then looked down and noticed Brownie sweetly staring up at me, as she took a leak on my pant leg. "Hey! Whatcha doing, girl? You couldn't find a tree?"

"Once you get peed on," Janelle swooned, "you

know it's love."

I hugged Janelle goodbye, and thanked her for sharing her heart-wrenching story. On the car ride home, as the sun set in the distance, I gazed over at Brownie riding shotgun beside me, head hanging out the window against the breeze, smiling ear to floppy ear. It suddenly dawned on me that for the first time in months, I was something that I hadn't been since Pete had passed away: happy.

CHAPTER 7
TRIPLE DOG DARE

Things were looking up in the Keefe household. Not only had I gotten the hang of this dog-fostering thing, I was motivated to start painting again. Of course Donny was thrilled with this development.

He dropped by the studio to see what I was working on, or maybe just to verify with his own eyes that I was functioning again, and was elated to discover my latest painting-in-progress—a large nine-by-four-feet-long triptych, featuring three panels of Brownie set against three different red, yellow, and green-tinted backgrounds. It might not have been my best work, but at least it was new work, and Donny was ecstatic.

"I love it. It's brilliant," he popped open a bottle of champagne. "Let's celebrate!"

"You're just buttering me up to justify your commission."

"Okay, brilliant might be an overstatement. It is a dog painting for God's sake," he qualified. "But it's a good solid piece and has a certain panache. What are you calling it?"

"Don't have a title yet."

"How about Three Dog Night?" he offered.

"Or Three Dog Day?" I shot back.

"Dog Day Afternoon," he one-upped me.

"Dog Days of Summer."

"Every Dog Has Its Days?"

"Triple Dog Dare Ya!"

"Fine, doesn't matter what you call it," Donny chortled. "I'm just glad to see you back at it. After all you've been through these last few months, it looks like your finally coming out of the tunnel to see the light. This dog's a real lifesaver."

"Yes, she is," I agreed, bending down to scrub Brownie's ears. "You saved Daddy, didn't you, girl? *Didn't youuuuuu?* Yes, you did!"

Brownie heartily wagged her tail, happy to contribute to help the team. But then I saw some movement out of the corner of my eye and glanced across the room to see Pete lying on the floor, taking a nap in his old favorite spot of sunlight, to my surprise. He didn't look peaceful though, a blood shot-eyed lump of heavy-breathing fur.

"What is it?" Donny sensed my distraction.

Speechless, I tried to form words to describe my second Pete sighting, but then Brownie began hacking and wheezing hysterically, choking on something.

"Brownie girl, you okay?" I rushed over to pry her mouth open and found Donny's champagne cork wedged in the back of her throat. I stuck my fingers down her gullet to pull the plug out from behind her molars. "Good job," I showed Donny the chewed cork. "You almost killed my dog."

"Here's to Brownie," Donny raised his glass for a toast. "She has magnificent taste!"

Relieved, I looked back at the patch of sunlight, but Pete was no longer there.

That night around ten, my cellphone chirped: *JANELLE CALLING.*

I picked up, "Hey, JJ. What's this, a booty call?"

"You wish. Listen, I have some good news or bad news, depending how you look at it. Remember Brownie's old foster family, the Fosters?"

"Huh?"

"The Fosters. They're the ones who were fostering Brownie before you—and their last name's Foster, too."

"O-kay," I nodded.

"Well, the Fosters just got returned from their vacation and now they want Brownie back."

"What do you mean they want her back?"

"They want to adopt her. Permanently," Janelle explained. "So you're off the hook."

My heart dropped, as I turned to Brownie nestled up on the couch beside me, neatly licking her paws. If this was good news, why did I feel sick to my stomach?

"Wait, is this another one of your cheap sales ploys?" I asked.

"No, I'm on my way to your house right now to come get her."

"What? They can't have her," I protested. "Brownie

is *my* dog."

"Charlie, you've had plenty of opportunities to adopt her, but didn't. These people are willing to make a lifetime commitment."

"Yeah, well, I already committed," I argued. "I took this dog when nobody else wanted her. I saved her from death row."

"I know. And we really appreciate all you did for Brownie."

"Great, thanks a lot, but now you're gonna take her away from me?"

"Charlie, don't you want what's best for Brownie? You had your chance."

"I know, but I'm new to this foster thing. I was going to make it official. Just didn't get around to filling out the paperwork."

"I'm sorry. It's too late. The Fosters are big donors and they already sent me a check for the deposit—okay, I'm here."

I jumped up to peek through the front curtains and saw Janelle's dog mobile van pull into my drive. Dropping the phone, I grabbed Brownie and raced outside onto the front porch to defend my property.

"I can't let you take her!" I informed Janelle, as she stepped out of the van. "Look at Brownie's face. She's traumatized!"

Truth be told, Brownie actually looked more amused than distressed by this hostage standoff.

"Charlie, please. Don't turn this into *Kramer vs. Kramer*, okay?"

"Screw you, it's not your dog!" I objected, and then made a run for it, dashing into the backyard lugging Brownie, as if we were fleeing a psychotic murderer in a scary horror flick.

"What are you doing?" Janelle stood there, unmoved by my childish response. "Where are you going?"

Brownie and I darted through the patio past the tool shed, and then ducked down behind Pete's rickety, old doghouse to wait it out until the coast was clear. I covered Brownie's mouth to keep her quiet, but then my cellphone started ringing, as the readout flashed: *JANELLE CALLING.*

Janelle followed the incessant noise of my ringtone, which quickly gave away our hiding spot, and calmly walked around back to find us stowed under the doghouse looking like two disheveled, dirt-stained fugitives.

"Charlie," she clicked off her phone, "you must be feeling awfully foolish about now."

"*Yeahhh*," I admitted, smushing my face up next to Brownie's, trying to make us look as cute and inseparable together as possible. "But love makes a guy do crazy things."

"Okay, so are you going to do the right thing and give Brownie back to me, so I can take her to her forever home?"

"No, this is her forever home," I said defiantly. "I want Brownie. I *need* Brownie. I know I wasn't ready before, but now I am."

"Are you saying what I think you're saying?" Janelle deepened her tone.

"Yes," I insisted. "I don't care how great these Foster people are. There's no way in hell I'm giving up Brownie. We're in love."

Janelle's eyebrows drooped, beleaguered. "Can I just say? I've adopted out over 1,800 dogs through my organization and this has never happened before. Are you willing to fully accept that Brownie is now your dog for keeps? Forever? Swear on Pete's grave?" she stipulated. "There's no going back after this."

"Yes," I pledged, holding up my right hand.

"Because my reputation is on the line here. I've already told the Fosters that Brownie was theirs and they are going to be heartbroken if they find out she's not."

"Tell them I'm very sorry, but I can't do it. This is my dog."

"I'll call them and try to explain the situation," Janelle repeated, "but you're going to owe me big for this."

"Whatever it takes," I said, showering Brownie with kisses. "Anything for my girl."

"Fine. Dinner Thursday at The Mission Ranch

Inn—your treat?"

Man, this woman didn't waste any time cashing in a favor.

"Okay," I played along, "as long as you don't mind sitting outside. I'll have to bring Brownie since I've noticed she's been having some separation anxiety lately."

"Are you sure that's not just you?" Janelle laughed.

I broke into a wide grin, as Brownie jumped into my lap, gratefully thumping her tail against my chest. This new dog was helping me bounce back in more ways than one. My heart was opening up again.

CHAPTER 8

DOG SPELLED BACKWARDS IS GHOST

The Mission Ranch Inn is a rustic, romantic comfort food restaurant. Unfortunately, the meal wasn't all that comforting since my stomach was tied in knots considering I hadn't been out on a real date in quite some time. Although calling it a date may have been presumptuous on my part. I couldn't discern if Janelle fancied this evening as a potential courtship, or just purely payback.

Sitting outside on the back terrace with a spectacular view of the meadow, the night started off precariously with Brownie playing the third wheel, constantly watching our every bite with her hypnotizing, give-me-some eyes from underneath the table. Janelle, being a dog person, was used to these shenanigans though. And she looked smashing in a sexy summer wrap dress. I had never seen her out of her standard dog-saving uniform of yoga pants and a hoodie, and she cleaned up nicely.

After ordering a bottle of Pinot, the wine flowed, as did the conversation. We talked openly about everything going on in our lives, except for dogs, which was a major milestone for us. Once we dove into dessert, she probed a little deeper.

"So, you know all about my love life. How come you're not with anyone?" she asked. "Is there something wrong with you? No offense, but a single guy over forty who's never been married? Not a good sign."

I choked on my cappuccino. She was nothing if not direct.

"Who said I was 40?" I retaliated. "Do I look that old?"

She turned silent.

"Kidding, I'm 42," I smiled. "But just because I've never been married and don't have a carload of kids doesn't mean I'm damaged goods."

"No, just less likely capable of having a deep, lasting relationship," she speculated.

"Maybe I've just had better luck with dogs than women."

"Whew, that's a relief. All the girls at the dog park thought you were neuter."

"What? Why would they think that?"

"Probably because you've never hit on any of them."

"That's because they're all married!" I contended.

"So? Married women love to get hit on. Makes them feel hot again," she added. "Plus you're an artiste with a King Charles Cavalier. Not exactly the most manly dog around."

We had a laugh, and I slipped Brownie another cookie under the table. Good thing I wasn't too insecure in my masculinity, because the soft, prissy image of my new pup obviously wasn't doing me any favors.

After dinner, we merrily strolled out to my car arm in arm, when we heard a robust voice shout, "Janelle!"

I looked across the parking lot to see a perfectly well-dressed husband, wife, and two kids walking toward us with a pair of German Shepherds.

"Hi, guys!" Janelle waved, and then tersely hissed at me. "Hurry up, let's go."

"What's the rush?"

"That's them," she grabbed Brownie and shoved her down into the backseat. "The Fosters!"

"The Fosters who fostered Brownie? Oh, I should go thank them—"

"No," Janelle yanked me into the car, as the model family crept closer. "Just go!"

"But why can't I say hi?"

"Because," she said, reaching over to turn the key in the ignition. "I lied to them about Brownie. I told them she got run over by a cement truck and died."

"*What?* Why?"

"I'll tell you later—just go. *Go, go, go!*"

I revved up the engine, and we peeled out of the lot right before the Fosters caught a glimpse of Brownie in back. After we got down the road out of sight, I pulled over to the shoulder.

"Why'd you lie to the Fosters about Brownie?" I asked. "What's the big deal? They already have two dogs."

"Because they're freaks."

"They didn't look very freaky to me."

"Okay, not freaky in the classical sense," Janelle rephrased it. "They're actually very nice people and donate a ton of moolah to the rescue. But. They have way too much money and they treat their dogs like accessories. They're always traveling, going off to Bali, or some exotic place all the time. And then they dump their dogs off on us as soon as they get sick and old, or tired of them. For all I know, they probably just wanted Brownie so their other dogs would have something to chew on."

I sat there, stunned. "Hold on, let me get this straight. So after knowing all that, you were still going to take Brownie away from me and give her to these Foster people anyway just because they give you a lot of money? Isn't that unethical?"

"Well, I was hoping it didn't come to that, but I had to use them as leverage to push you to make a decision," she maintained. "I'll do anything to find my dogs a home. And that includes putting the pressure on our more commitment-phobic foster parents. Sometimes you have to shit or get off the pot."

"Man, what kind of dog racket are you running, lady?" I mocked her, reaching back to pat Brownie on the head. "You little scammer."

Be that as it may, I couldn't help but admire Janelle's ballsy salesmanship. She knew how to get what she wanted in this world.

"Chill out," she sparred. "You're the big winner here. You've got yourself a great dog. But if you're still not satisfied, I'll be happy to throw in a bonus prize to seal the deal."

"Like what?"

She leaned in closer and gave me a long, wet, tasty kiss.

"Does that come with a month supply of dog food?" I joked.

"Sure. Let's go back to your place so I can confirm your address," she flirted seductively.

And with that, we got back on the road and sped off for home. If this dog was going to reward me with an adult play date, I wasn't above redeeming the offer.

Needless to say, I broke several speed limit laws racing back to the house. And Brownie was pleased to be left alone with the doggie bag of leftovers, as Janelle and I hustled into the bedroom to savor our own post-dinner treat. I'm not a kiss-and-tell guy, so I won't go into all the sordid details, but it's safe to say that we tore into each other with the type of wild animal passion that can only happen between two people who met at a dog park. Perhaps we were unwittingly inspired from all those afternoons watching our favorite charges going at it with such reckless abandon.

But then something quite extraordinary happened. And it had nothing to do with sex. Some might call it magical, others may deem it demonic. I wouldn't have believed it myself if I hadn't seen it with my own eyes. While Janelle and I were entangled in embrace, I heard something jangle and whirled around to see a ghost-like version of Pete—that's right, my old dead dog— standing in the doorway eyeing me with a smug look on his face, something he always did to show his contempt whenever I brought strangers home.

Pete, is that you? I rubbed my eyes to focus on this feral figment of my imagination. And then he spoke:

"Hey, man. Good to see you back on the horse again," Pete snickered. "*Yeeee-hawww!*"

"Shit!" I squealed, falling off the mattress, and crashing onto the floor.

"What's wrong?" Janelle sat up, alarmed.

"Dude, don't freak," the ghost of Pete went on. "I know you thought you lost me forever, but I'm back."

I stared aghast at this odd, new supernatural Pete in disbelief. Was I seeing things again? Who was this beast? Could my beloved ex-dog be talking to me? And why did he have such a crass, raspy voice? Back when Pete was alive, I imagined that if he could talk that his voice would sound like a charming, debonair, upper- class British gent, say, Cary Grant or Michael Caine—

but this frizzy scoundrel sounded more like a street thug from a Scorsese film.

"Charlie! Are you all right?" Janelle leaned over the bed with concern.

"It's, ummm, my dog," I sputtered.

"I know, isn't it adorable? She's in hog heaven," Janelle said, looking over fondly at Brownie bundled in her dog bed, wolfing down the leftovers.

"Yo, what's up with that bitch?" Pete chimed in.

"Hey, watch your mouth!" I snarled back, to Janelle's confusion.

"No, not the girl—I meant the bimbo King Charles puppy over there," Pete heckled. "Didn't take you long to move on."

"Charlie," Janelle interrupted, "who are you talking to?"

"*Pete*," I pointed emphatically at my old dog. "Can't you see him?"

She looked at me preposterously, so I turned back to show her the newfangled glow-in-the-dark Pete, but he disappeared.

"Are you feeling okay?" Janelle glared at me insanely. "You're white as a sheet."

"Wow, think I've had too much to drink," I babbled. "I just had this really odd visual pop in my head."

"Oh my god, were you thinking of someone else when you were with me?" Janelle's cheeks reddened.

"Yes," I stammered, but this didn't go over well judging by the scowl on Janelle's face. "I mean, no. No!"

Sure, there had been times in my hookup history when I thought of other things during sexual intercourse as a diversion to help prolong the enjoyment, such as football scores or stock prices—but never dogs. And certainly not Pete. That was taboo.

"Charlie, if you're not ready for this, just tell me," Janelle put her clothes back on. "I'm a big girl. I can take it."

But I couldn't say anything because I didn't know if I was just having performance anxiety, or an anxiety attack.

Then the mirage of Pete popped up again outside the closet. "I can't believe it. This is who you chose as my replacement?" he questioned, then brazenly swiped Brownie's food scraps. "*Haaaaaa*, like stealing candy from a baby!"

"Did you see that?" I asked Janelle, nodding back at Pete.

"See what?" Janelle replied, at a loss.

"Don't waste your time," Pete intervened. "She can't see me or hear me. Only you can. And maybe your new hussy here since we are technically related," he grunted mischievously, giving Brownie a noogie.

"Why not?" I quibbled.

"Hello? Boo. I'm a ghost. And 'cuz I wasn't her dog."

"We have to talk," I herded Pete into the bathroom, shielding him from Janelle's view, which didn't make sense since she couldn't see him anyway.

"Charlie, what are you doing?" Janelle interjected. "You're acting really weird."

"I know, I know, just give me a sec to straighten this out."

"Screw this. I'm out of here," Janelle got up to leave.

"No, don't go," I begged, giving her my best puppy dog eyes. "I'll be right back. Please?"

She sat back down on the bed, aggravated.

"Stay, *stayyyyyy*..." I motioned to her, as I kicked Pete into the bathroom, shutting the door behind us so we could talk man-to-dog or man-to-ghost, or whatever this creature was.

"Finally. Alone at last," Pete declared, and then recognized his old plastic cone sitting on an upper shelf like a tarnished trophy. "What'd you keep that for? That thing still gives me nightmares!"

"What the—?" I said, still not believing my eyes and ears. "Who are you?"

"I told you. It's me, Pete—your dog, your boy, your BFF."

"But you're not a dog. You can talk. Dogs can't talk!" I yelped, and then lowered my voice, so as not to frighten Janelle any more than she had been already.

"All right, I'm more than just a dog," Pete

attempted to explain. "You always said I was one of a kind."

"But you're dead!"

"I know, thanks for burning me up. Getting cremated is not cool. Hey, but I still look good, don't I?" he pranced and preened, pumping out his chest, flexing his arms. "Check out these guns."

Then there was a knock on the door.

"Charlie, you okay in there?" Janelle called from the other side.

"Yes," I answered, while Pete simultaneously blared, "*NO!*"

"Shut up!" I restrained him.

"Don't sweat it," Pete muttered. "She can't hear me."

"You're scaring me," Janelle echoed. "Is there anything I can do to help? Should I call 911?"

"No, don't call anybody. I'll be right there," I tried to placate her. "Just having a little heart-to heart. With myself."

"How much longer are you gonna be?"

"One minute, I promise."

"Okay," she simmered, "but the clock's ticking."

"You know what? I like her," Pete remarked. "I 'member her from the dog park. She was always so nice. Had lotsa treats. And a good rack, too."

"What the hell's going on?" I grabbed the Pete clone and slammed him up against the wall. "Who sent you here?"

"Nobody sent me. I told ya, I'm a ghost," Pete proclaimed. "Dog spelled backwards isn't God. It's ghost. G-O-S-T."

"Ghost is G-H-O-S-T, not G-O-S-T," I corrected him.

"Whatever. I can talk, but I can't spell."

I gave up fighting it and slumped down on the floor, dumbfounded and disturbed.

"C'mon, man, I thought you'd be happy to see me," Pete sat down beside me.

"I am, I just don't understand. How could my old dog come back reincarnated as a ghost...that talks? It doesn't make sense," I told him. "How do I know it's really you?"

"Okay," Pete softened with a sentimental glimmer in his eye, "you wanna know why I'm here? I don't wanna get all mushy on ya, but I came back to say goodbye. We had a lotta fun times, but we never got to, y'know, end it on a positive note. So here I am."

I straightened up and looked deeply into this talking dog's eyes—and right then it didn't matter if he was a ghost, or a drug-induced illusion. He had me at goodbye.

"It's really you, Pete, isn't it?" I broke down blubbering. "It's really *you*."

"C'mere, ya big lug," Pete grinned, and I hugged the furry phantom, or what I could of him.

"Sorry I wasn't there for you at the end," I said regretfully. "I never would've gone to Paris if I knew you weren't gonna be here when I got back."

"It's okay. No worries," Pete forgave me, as my tears soaked his ghoulish fur. "I'm sorry, too, for crapping in your shoe that first day you brought the new puppy home."

"I knew that was you!" I laughed, and we pounded fists like schoolboy chums. "Was that also you I saw disguised as a coyote—and then later taking a nap in the studio?"

"I didn't wanna scare you, so I took it slow. Break you in easy first. You know, the coyote is a symbol of the trickster!"

Then we heard some noise coming from the other room.

"Okay, sit tight. I better go check on JJ—"

Overjoyed, I threw open the door to try and clear up this madness with Janelle, but was disheartened to find that she had already left, leaving behind a cherry red lipstick mark on Brownie's furrowed brow, along with a note tucked under her paw:

Charlie,
Thanks again for dinner. Sorry to leave without
saying goodbye, but it sounds like you have some
other issues to work out.

xo Janelle

My heart sank. I tried catching Janelle on her cell and sent her several texts, but they all went unanswered. I was unsure whether to be happy or sad. I'd just gotten back in touch with my old dead dog, but had lost the possible woman of my dreams.

Later, I went to bed that evening with Brownie sleeping on my arm and thoughts of Pete dancing in my head. This wasn't my ideal fantasy of a threesome, but it beat sleeping alone. And I slept better that night than I had in years.

CHAPTER 9
OLD DOG, NEW TRICKS

The morning after, I woke up rejuvenated with a new outlook on life. And since that apparition of Pete was nowhere to be seen, I reckoned that maybe his surprise cameo appearance last night was just a crazy dream after all. Pete coming back to life as a precocious talking dog? How ridiculous was that? Sometimes the mind does play tricks.

After Brownie and I returned from our dog walk of shame in my robe and slippers, I took my coffee into the studio to watch the sunrise—and there was a sight to behold. But not a pretty one. Strewn all over the room, torn to shreds, was the three-panel triptych painting of Brownie that I had recently finished. It was such a mess. It looked like a band of wolves had broken into my studio in the middle of the night and thrown a rave party. There was only one dog I knew who was capable of inflicting this much damage.

"Rough night last night, huh, boss?" I jumped and looked down to see Pete lounging beneath my easel, threads of canvas stuck to his chin.

"Hey, don't take it personal. We both know it wasn't your best," Pete deadpanned. "Now this is what I call a masterpiece," he surmised, strutting over to admire a portrait of himself leaning against the wall.

"Eat your heart out, Mona Lisa!"

"Pete," I dropped my coffee cup, and it smashed onto the floor. "You really are back."

"For realsies!" Pete whooped, as he sidled up next to Brownie chowing down on her breakfast kibble. "Hey, baby, whaddaya say me and you go slurp down some spaghetti and meatballs *Lady and the Tramp*-style?"

Brownie growled at Pete's aura, and then scurried away like a scaredy-cat. Apparently she, too, could see this new ghost of my old dog, which accounted for why she'd been acting so squeamish lately.

"These pups today," Pete huffed. "No respect."

"Like you should talk. You were afraid of your own shadow when I first brought you home."

"So what? I'm not ashamed. Below this badass exterior lies a sensitive, soulful terrier," Pete gloated.

I picked up the shredded tufts of canvas sprinkled everywhere. Pete may not have been an authority on art, but he was spot on about my Brownie painting. Even though there wasn't much left of it now, one thing was clear: I could do better than this. I then heard some rustling and turned to see Pete taunting Brownie, relishing his newfound role as the annoying older brother.

"Want a salmon crunchy, sweetcakes? *Yeahhh*, you know you want it," Pete teased, holding a snack above Brownie's nose, just out of her reach. "Go fetch!"

Pete faked throwing the treat across the room several times and Brownie chased after it, coming up baffled and empty-handed every time. "Dude, got yourself a real Einstein here," Pete stopped sarcastically. "She's so dumb, I've taken bowel movements smarter than her."

Then Pete either burped or farted, or did both at the same time, and blamed Brownie for it, cackling, "*Ewww*, Brownie, knock it off. That's gross!"

Good god, I shuddered to myself. My beloved old Pete is back—and not only is he a ghost, he's a boor, too.

"Speak of the devil," Donny greeted me, as I barged into the gallery, while he was busy hobnobbing a pair of well-heeled women, pouring them glasses of sparkling wine. "Barbara, Nancy, this is Charlie Keefe. The artist."

The ladies politely took in my slovenly t-shirt and flip-flops. They probably wouldn't have stopped to give me a nickel if I had passed by them on the street.

"Mister Keefe, we're huge dog lovers," the older one tittered. "I have two Goldens at home: Strawberry and Platinum. Both blondes."

I smiled preoccupied, glancing back out the front window at Brownie tied to a parking meter, while the ghost of Pete flaunted around her, trying to bait the young lass into eating some crud off the sidewalk.

"By the way, Charlie, I just sold that new painting of yours," Donny boasted, to whet the women's appetites.

"Which one?" I asked.

"The Brownie triptych," Donny elaborated. "I put some jpegs of it up on the website last night, and a German collector contacted me this morning to buy it."

"Um, you might want to cancel that," I shrank. "My dog ate it."

"You're joking, right?"

I nodded my head, nope.

"You're telling me your dog ate your homework?" Donny mused, stifling his disappointment in front of the women.

"Not just any dog," I answered, my eyes drifting to Pete and Brownie outside, leery of leaving them alone for too long. "Can we talk in back? It's kind of an emergency."

"Excuse us, ladies. Feel free to browse, and don't hesitate if you have any questions," Donny apprised our visitors, as we shuffled into the back office.

"That was rude," he scolded me. "You know who those women are? Two of the biggest philanthropists in Dallas. You're supposed to seduce our customers, not scare them away!"

"I've got a problem," I confessed. "A talking dog problem."

"Beg your pardon?"

"It's Pete," I said, anxiously peeking out the window to make sure he and Brownie were still there. "He's back."

"What do you mean he's back?"

"Back from the dead. He's *alive*. Well, not like us. He's a ghost. And he's living in my house."

"Oh, boy," Donny ogled me like a mental patient.

"Look, see for yourself. He's standing outside with Brownie," I dragged him over to the window. "Uh oh, you might not be able to see him because Pete says only I can because I'm his owner."

Donny peered out at Brownie canoodling any passerby who gave her the time of day. He would've seen Pete, too, if he could see ghosts, but he couldn't, and so he didn't.

"You're right. I can't see him," Donny took a slug of wine. "Have you been drinking this morning?"

"No, I'm serious!" I bellowed, our squabble drawing the attention of the Dallas art queens standing outside the doorway.

"Hey, you talkin' about me? My ears were burning," I heard Pete's voice ring out, and then saw my pet ghost materialize, lifting his leg to piss on Donny's treasured Rodin sculpture.

"Don't pee on that," I shooed him away. "It's a Rodin!"

"Looks like it could use a polish," Pete sneered.

"What are you doing?" Donny questioned, as I

blotted his sculpture dry with a napkin.

"Sorry, it's Pete. He was about to take a whiz on your Rodin, but I stopped him."

"Come here," Donny got in my face. "Let me smell your breath."

"Get away," I pushed him back.

"No, we both know you can't hold your liquor."

"I'm not drunk—I'm grieving!" I shouted, ruffling the chic ladies' feathers nearby.

Pete, sensing danger in the pack, jumped up between us and belched in Donny's face, letting out a foul scent that could only be described as death warmed over.

"Ugh, that's rancid," Donny recoiled in disgust. "What did you have for lunch—garlic toast and ass?"

"No, it's not me," I defended myself. "It's Pete!"

"Oh, please, Charlie. Stop blaming that damn dog for all your problems!"

The Dallas duo, meanwhile, had heard enough of our boisterous altercation and fled for the exit.

"Wait," Donny ran after them, shoving a sweaty business card into their affluent hands. "Don't leave. Here's our website. Can I get you some more wine?"

"No thanks, buh-bye!" the younger one clucked, as she and her cultured cohort quickly hightailed it out the door.

"Classy," Donny marched back to me, displeased. "Real smooth."

"*Ahhh*, shut your pie-hole," Pete snapped back.

"Pete, stop it."

"No, we put this gallery on the map," Pete persisted. "If it wasn't for us, this phony here would still be selling Thomas Kinkade knockoffs!"

"Don't worry, I'll handle this," I pulled him back. "Go wait outside with your sister."

"This buffoon doesn't get it. We're the talent here—"

"Leave. Now."

"*O-kayyyy*," Pete moped out the door.

"And don't pick on Brownie!" I called after him, and then whispered to Donny. "I tell you, he's like a two-year-old. He gets so jealous."

"I am *not* jealous!" Pete poked his muzzle through the front window.

"Charlie, I know this has been a stressful time for you. For *all* of us," Donny sat me down, disquieted by the bickering. "I've been so focused on the business lately that I ignored all the warning signs. But we're going to get you the best help money can buy."

I looked at Donny and could tell he was genuinely concerned about me, even if he didn't truly understand the predicament I was in. But then again, who could?

"Alissa has some doctor friends who might be able to refer you to a specialist who handles this type of thing," Donny suggested.

"Thanks, but I don't need a doctor," I said. "I need

someone who makes x-ray glasses for ghosts, so you can see what I see."

I glanced back out the window and saw Pete trying to mount Brownie from behind. "Okay, good talk, Donny. Gotta go!"

I raced outside and smacked Pete on the rump to discipline him. "Pete, stop humping your sister!" I harped, untying Brownie from the parking meter. "Have some respect."

"What?" Pete wrangled. "I was teaching her a lesson. She was acting like a 'ho, licking anything that walked by. You think she only loves you? She loves *everybody*."

"Aw, c'mere, girl," I picked up Brownie and cradled her in my arms, covering her soft, droopy ears from Pete's onslaught. "Don't listen to your brother. You're my sweet little Brownie fudge cake and that's all you'll ever be, okay, baby?"

Brownie giddily licked my nose with affection, as Pete sorely glowered at us.

"Don't be a sourpuss," I joshed Pete. "We're all family now."

"Yeah, but I'm still your favorite, right?" Pete grunted.

I unlocked the car, and we hopped in to go grab an early supper.

"Shotgun!" Pete roared, nudging Brownie into the backseat, as we headed back for home to share our first sit-down meal together as a unit. This made it official. I was a two dog man now.

CHAPTER 10
THE FIRST DOG IS THE DEEPEST

We barely got through dinner without a food fight breaking out, as Brownie and Pete stuffed their faces on hamburgers and hot dogs like two contestants at a Fourth of July eating contest. I don't know what having kids is like, but if this was any indication, then cooking for them is being a chef, bouncer, and babysitter all rolled into one. And even though Pete could somehow still digest food as a ghost, he was conveniently unable to help with the dishes.

After supper, we retired to the living room for a nightcap. There just so happened to be a Ghost Story Marathon playing on TV; we missed *The Blair Witch Project*, *Poltergeist*, and *The Sixth Sense*, but turned it on just in time to see *All Dogs Go To Heaven*. Coincidence? I think not. Even so, the plot line was too close to the bone for Pete's taste, so we shut it off.

"Pathetic," Pete bellyached at the sight of Brownie crashed asleep in my lap, tuckered out from putting up with his antics all day. "You've spoiled that dog rotten."

"Look who's talking. Didn't hear you complaining about all the treats and attention I smothered you with for years."

"Yeah, only after I trained ya. When you first got me, you didn't know what you were doing. Made me sleep in a banana box outside for a week."

"I did?" I smiled, forgetting that failure from my dog parenting past.

"Hell yeah, froze my tushy off out there. This new girl should be grateful to me. I paved the way through a lotta crap so she could have this pampered life."

"Well, being the first dog is always the hardest," I agreed.

With Brownie conked out, this finally gave Pete and I a chance to really talk. We stayed up all night chewing the fat as if we were two undergrads fueled on coffee and cigarettes, except our elixirs of choice were beef jerky and that bottle of barrel-aged tawny port that Donny had gifted me. The port went down smooth, warming our bellies on this chilly night like a magic potion, as I had many questions for my old friend, topics ranging from how dogs perceive time to Pete's personal thoughts on toilet bowl water.

Eventually, we moved onto some deeper questions that had been nagging me. "So, on that last day, were you mad at me for having Doctor Paula put you to sleep?" I asked.

"Nah, it had to be done," Pete looked me dead in the eye. "I was eighteen. You know how old that is in dog years?"

"Really? I thought you were only fifteen or sixteen. That's what they told me at the pound."

"It don't matter. Age is just a number. But I was

long in the tooth, that's for sure," Pete groaned. "Getting old sucked. I couldn't keep up anymore. My body was falling apart. Couldn't see or hear worth a damn. Sense of smell went to shit. I couldn't wag my tail without getting a cramp!"

"Were you in a lot of pain at the end?"

"Yeah, I was not a happy camper," Pete admitted. "Remember that time you left the giant chocolate bunny out on the coffee table for Easter and I ate it all? Then I started puking up marshmallow, so we had to go get my stomach pumped?"

"I'm still paying off that vet bill," I cringed.

"It felt like that, but about a gazillion times worse. I didn't wanna die, but when I started losing my desire for food, I knew it was time to go."

"I'm sorry you had to go through all that," I said, teary-eyed. As hard as this was to hear, I knew it was the truth. "Other dog owners told me that dogs give you a look when they're ready to go. But you never gave me The Look. I kept looking for The Look, but I didn't get The Look."

"No, I gave you The Look," Pete insisted. "Trust me. Lotsa times."

"You did? What's The Look look like? Show me."

"No."

"Why not?"

"Because it's out of context," Pete alleged. "You can't fake it."

"Come on, do it for me. Just once. I need this. For my own peace of mind."

Pete grumbled and closed his eyes to concentrate, then broke into a grim, humorless gaze.

"That's it? That's The Look?" I replied. "It just looks like you're bored."

"Sorry, it's been a while," Pete frowned, trying to do The Look again. "Okay, how 'bout this?" he flashed another dreary stare, but it still wasn't very emotive. Like a bad actor, Pete just looked slightly more grumpy than usual.

"I'm not feeling it," I said.

"Whatever, I can't do The Look on command. It just happens," Pete gave up. "Don't be sorry for how it ended. I had a good life. Can't complain."

I nodded, satisfied, but then Pete continued, "Okay, yeah, do I wish you would've taken me out more to go play? Heck yes. It got dull sitting inside all the time watching your paint dry."

"I had to work," I said. "How do you think I could afford to bring home all that bacon for you?"

"You asked, so I'm just tellin' ya. Life doesn't go on forever. It's over in a heartbeat. And if you don't take time to get out and look around every once in a while, you're gonna end up trapped inside your own head and miss all the good stuff."

"So, is there really such a thing as heaven?" I asked him. "Or did you just go to doggie heaven?"

"You really wanna know what happens after you die?" Pete leaned in with a devilish smirk.

"Yes," I slid to the edge of my seat, and even Brownie's ears perked up for this.

Pete took a swig of his port, and then shrugged, "Sorry, man. Can't tell ya. It's against the rules."

"Rules?" I gasped. "What rules?"

"The heaven thing's a big deal. I could get in a lotta trouble if I told you. I've probably said too much already."

"Come on, Pete, throw the dog a bone. It's me. Your *master*. What's the purpose of coming back from the dead if you can't give me some answers to life's biggest questions?" I pleaded.

"Wish I could, but I can't," he explained. "I'm just a messenger of dog—this is the Holy Ghost we're talkin' about! If I told you, they might not let me back in. And believe me, heaven's the kinda place you don't wanna lose your membership to. All I can say is it's pretty doggone nice."

"Nice? That's it? Nicer than what—Hawaii?"

"You'll find out for yourself someday, my friend," Pete laughed off my cross-examination. "If you don't screw it up first."

This wasn't very reassuring. Here I was chomping at the bit to learn some meaningful life lessons, but all Pete was giving me was trite kindergarten common sense.

"Hey, but you know what's really cool?" he intimated. "When I was up there, I gotta party with some big-time famous dogs like Old Yeller, Benji, and Spuds MacKenzie—the Bud Light dog. Spuds is a real meathead. He's still stuck in the '80s."

Just then, a jolt of thunder rocked the house, rattling our glasses, as streaks of lightning carved up the night sky.

"Okay, I think that means I better shut up," Pete jumped up skittishly, heeding a sign from above. "That's all, folks!"

I slung Brownie over my shoulder and off to beddy-bye we went. As I turned off all the lights and tiptoed down the hallway following Pete's trail, I began to wonder: if there is such a thing as heaven, maybe I was already there?

CHAPTER 11
LET TALKING DOGS LIE

I've never been a fan of talking dog movies, but now that we had a real-life talking dog in the family, the benefits were starting to grow on me.

For one, you always know where you stand. There are no mixed messages, or worrisome behaviors, to cause misunderstandings. If the talking dog is happy, he belts out corny pop songs; if he's mad, he cusses like a longshoreman; if he's hungry, he gobbles the steak right off your plate. At least that's how Pete behaved around us. Who says a dead dog can't teach you new tricks?

And what's more, this ghostly Pete thrived in his new big brother role, taking Brownie under his wing to show her the ways of the dog world, as well as how to manipulate her daddy. He taught her how to train me to take her for longer walks, buy her more goodies at the pet shop, and heap larger servings into her food bowl. Granted, it didn't take a genius to push the right buttons since I was such a soft touch.

Pete was also very helpful because he could translate Brownie's minor ailments and allergies that were previously impossible for me to detect. This, of course, didn't stop him from busting my balls, as he wasn't shy about expressing his views on my life with "The Rebound Dog", as he cynically called Brownie.

"Dude, don't baby her. Make her work for it," Pete goaded me at the dog park after I had tossed Brownie a treat, even though she hadn't moved a muscle to fetch a tennis ball I'd thrown to her. "I used to have to run to Tijuana and back to get a treat out of you. This chick just tilts her head and you give her the whole bag."

"So what, you're saying I'm a bad parent?" I asked Pete. "I know I made some mistakes, but I did the best I could."

"These pups today," Pete took in the other breeds zigzagging across the field in their designer doggie duds and play gear. "When I was their age—"

"Yeah, yeah, we know, you used to have to walk five miles through the ice and snow to get to school every day."

Then a gang of unleashed mutts came running over to sniff Pete's backside, which irritated him.

"Yo, scram! Get outta here!" Pete woofed.

"Can those dogs see you?" I asked, considering that Brownie had been the only dog to show any reaction to him so far.

"Beats me," Pete whapped them away with his tail.

"Sadie! Willow! Come here!" a female voice called, and I recognized it immediately, as Janelle walked up with five more used dogs in tow. My heart jumped. I hadn't seen her since the night Pete had magically reappeared.

"Hi, Charlie," she smiled.

"Uh-oh, here we go again," Pete cajoled. "Okay, you distract her with some witty banter—and I'll steal her bacon strips."

"Pipe down," I hissed. "How are you, JJ? I tried calling you, but I never heard back."

"I know. It just got so crazy the last time I saw you," she said. "I thought you were having a nervous breakdown."

"Yeah, I probably would've left, too," I conceded, and then saw Pete sneaking up behind Janelle to dip his snout into her side pocket for snacks.

"Pete, don't!" I swatted him away, rattling Janelle.

"Charlie?" she backed off timidly.

"Sorry, didn't mean to frighten you," I tried to cover. "I just, well, there's something I need to tell you."

"Like what? You're seeing ghosts of your dead dog?" I looked at her in disbelief. Could she see Pete as well? "Donny called last night and told me everything."

My posture crumbled, and then I noticed the other dog owners standing ten feet away, talking in hushed tones. Now it all made sense. I thought I'd seen a few of them pulling their dogs away earlier when I moseyed in with Brownie. If the dog park people knew my deep, dark, crazy secret, it would spread through town faster than the flu.

"Great," I caved. "Donny told you?"

"Don't be mad at him. He's just worried about you," Janelle stated matter-of-factly.

"Yeah, who gives a crap what these people think?" Pete butted in to join our discussion. "They have their own problems. Like that one over there? Cheating on her husband. Her friend there's a closet hoarder. And the bald guy with the Rhodesian Ridgeback? His condo's getting foreclosed on Monday."

"How do you know all this?" I turned to Pete.

"I'm enlightened. I can smell it another galaxy away."

"Wow, your interior life must be fascinating with all those voices and visions going on inside your head," Janelle furrowed her brow.

"Such is the life of an artist," I sighed.

"So is *he* here now?" she asked.

"Who?"

"Pete."

"Yeah, he's right beside you," I affirmed.

Being a good sport, she knelt down and mimicked petting the outline of a small dog.

"No, on your left," I said.

Janelle, to her credit, kept at it, doing her best to connect with my unearthly ex-pet. "I think I feel him. It's much warmer and tingly right here in this area."

"Whoo, I love this girl!" Pete giggled, ticklish. "Lower, lower..."

"Don't be a slimeball," I chastised Pete, then smiled back at Janelle. "It's okay, you can't see him because he's not your dog. That's what Pete says. Some kind of bizarre ghost dog logic."

"I've never told anyone this before, but I keep pictures of all my old dogs that have passed away hung up over my bed," Janelle revealed. "To watch over me at night and protect me. Does that sound cuckoo?"

"You're asking me?" I chuckled, which brought some much needed levity to the situation. This spiritual charade might have seemed pointless on the surface, but it did draw us closer. "Look, I know I was an idiot the other night, but maybe I could make up for it and cook you dinner this week?"

"Oh, Charlie, Charlie, Charlie..." Janelle deliberated. "I think you're a really sweet guy—"

"But?"

"I have my own dog issues. I have to pick up a truckload of fosters from Salinas tomorrow. And my webmaster just quit, so now I have to find another IT guy to update the database. And as much as I like you— and, er, Pete here," she glanced down to acknowledge my ghost, "I just can't deal with this right now. Have you researched if there's any medication you can take for this?"

"For what—seeing talking dogs?" I retorted, as a bunch of Janelle's dogs returned to hassle Pete.

"Back off, boys," Pete growled, not enamored with their company. "Don't make me angry. You wouldn't like me when I'm angry."

Janelle's crew ignored Pete's warning, and began

circling him, snipping and snarling at his hair-raising presence.

"Sadie! Rico! What are you guys doing?" Janelle sniped.

"I think they see Pete," I said.

"How?"

"I don't know, but if dogs can predict earthquakes and other natural disasters, then seeing ghosts must not seem all that crazy."

Pete, however, wasn't in the mood to socialize, and flashed his fangs at the foster dogs. "I'm warnin' ya: my bite's worse than my bark."

"Better call your dogs off," I alerted Janelle. "Pete's not enjoying this."

"Don't be silly," she simpered. "They're just playing around."

But then one of Janelle's rescue dogs, Max, a fifty pound retriever mix, stuck his nose in too close, and before the docile fella knew what hit him—the ghost of Pete clamped down on the scruff of the bigger dog's neck and picked him up off the ground, shaking him like a rag doll.

Janelle watched in horror, as from her viewpoint all she could see was poor Max flying around in mid-air, as if he was a tetherball being walloped back and forth by some invisible satanic force.

"Max?" she screamed, shielding her eyes. "*MAXXXXX!*"

"Pete, stop!" I cried. "Let go!"

"He started it!" Pete muffled.

"*Let him go!*" I hollered, and Pete harmlessly flung Max off to the side into a patch of weeds. Max jumped up whimpering and rushed over to cower between Janelle's legs, as Brownie casually waddled up to see what all the fuss was about.

"Thanks for the backup, sis," Pete scoffed at Brownie.

"Maxie boy, are you okay?" Janelle inspected him thoroughly for puncture wounds, but couldn't find any evidence of a dog bite. She gaped back in Pete's direction, flabbergasted. "Omigosh, was that...*Pete?*"

"I warned 'em," Pete said ruthlessly, spitting out dog hair, shades of *Rambo*. "They drew first blood. Not me."

"Yeah," I said, to answer Janelle's question. "Pete's very sorry." I shot him a stern look of parental disapproval. "Bad ghost dog. Very bad."

Janelle eyeballed us in awe, but I couldn't tell if she was a believer, or just bamboozled. "Well, nice seeing you again, Charlie, but I better get back to work."

She gathered her precious cargo of dogs into the back of her van and quickly split. Watching her go, I turned to Pete, exasperated. As much as I always thought of him as my own personal savior, he could sometimes be a little devil.

"Why'd you have to beat up her dog?" I harassed

Pete. "I mean, was that necessary? I really like that girl."

Pete, not the least bit remorseful, hacked up a thick hairball onto the asphalt pavement. "That's what you get for messin' with a ghost."

CHAPTER 12
THE GHOST DOG WHISPERER

The rush from all that dog park excitement had worn off by the time we made it back to the house where we were surprised to discover Donny, Alissa, and her friend waiting for us inside.

"Hi, Charlie, have a seat," Donny advised as Brownie, Pete, and I strode through the front door.

"Not this bozo again," Pete grimaced. Even cute, little easygoing Brownie let out a snide grumble.

"What's going on, Donny? Last time I checked, this was my house," I said, closing the door. "Did you at least offer your guests a glass of wine?"

"No thanks, we're fine," Donny declined.

"Wow, don't think I've heard you turn down free vino before. Are you feeling okay?"

"Charlie, this is for you," Donny clasped his hands. "This is an intervention. A doggie intervention."

"Is that so?" I rolled my eyes. "Thanks for telling Janelle and everybody at the dog park about Pete. Now the whole town knows."

"Charlie—"

"I told you that privately. As a friend."

"That's why I'm here," Donny tried to appease me. "That's why we're *all* here. To show our support. You know Alissa, and this is her friend, Sofi," he introduced a pleasant, middle-aged Middle Eastern woman, clothed in a long, loose-fitting floral top. "Sofi's a medium-slash-exorcist. She clears away evil spirits out of people's houses."

"Forgive me for interrupting, but I prefer *exorciser*," Sofi corrected Donny. "Exorcist has such a negative connotation because of that dreadful movie with the girl vomiting, spinning her head."

While Sofi appeared to be a decent person who took her craft seriously, I still didn't want her in my house—especially since she had been recommended by Alissa, Donny's spouse who, though kindhearted, was often poorly misguided in her attempts at spiritual growth, having been swindled in the past by scores of bogus yogis, immoral gurus, and other New Age hucksters.

"So, Charlie, we've told Sofi all about your little Pete problem," Alissa volunteered.

"What Pete problem? I don't have any problem with Pete."

"Yeah, you're the one we've got a problem with," Pete spat, bounding up into the recliner to get a front row seat.

"We're not here to attack you," Alissa gently caressed Brownie. "We're here to help you. And Brownie, too."

"Yes, because Brownie's tired of being possessed by ghosts, aren't you, sweetie pie?" Donny mocked, placing his ear up to Brownie's lips so he could feign listening to her speak. "I know, ghosts are *scaryyyy.*"

"Don't be a dick," I ripped Donny.

"What? If Pete can talk, why can't Brownie? Where's her voice? Who's speaking up for her? She has a dog in this fight, too."

"Brownie can't talk. She's just a dog!" I erupted. "Look, I'm not making this up. I appreciate you wanting to help, but this is my problem—not yours. And I'll deal with it my way."

"Sir, do you have a picture of your doggie that I could see?" Sofi queried. "The one that passed?"

"Take your pick," I said, waving at the plethora of Pete paintings decorating the walls.

"Not that one," Pete carped, as Sofi looked closely at a degrading portrait of him dressed up in an orange pumpkin-shaped fleece for Halloween. "I hate that picture. So emasculating."

"So, do you have a successful track record communicating with dogs from the dead?" I asked Sofi.

"No, I predominantly work with the spirits of human beings that have passed, but I've been hired to contact animals as well. A couple horses, and a parrot once. Mostly cats."

"Figures. Pussy lover," Pete cracked.

"Hey!" I signaled Pete to keep his mouth shut.

"It is quite natural for those close to their pets to project human qualities onto them," Sofi philosophized, shadowing her hands over the painting of Pete, tracing the contours of his body with her fingertips, trying to correspond with him through the work of art. "And I can tell that Pete held a very deep place in your heart. Such a suave, gentle, clever animal. Quite exceptional for a dog."

"Man, this psycho really knows her shit," Pete blushed.

I, however, wasn't so charmed by her vague Clairvoyant 101 assessment. Yeah, so what? I thought. Anybody who visited the gallery or clicked on our website could've told me that.

"Now I want you to pass on a message to Pete from me. Tell him there's nothing to fear. I come in peace," Sofi announced, lighting a bundle of twigs and sage with a match. "And tell him that he has been a wonderful dog to you and fulfilled his service time here on Earth, and his spirit is now free to go," she then started chanting gibberish, walking room to room swinging the sage, releasing a smoky green haze throughout the house. Pete started gagging from all the smoke, as did Brownie, Donny, and Alissa.

"I don't know," I stewed, the smell of incense making me nauseous. "This doesn't feel right. Pete's not that spiritual."

"Is this stuff toxic?" Donny questioned, coughing up phlegm.

"No, it's all natural," Sofi claimed. "One hundred-percent organic."

"I'm not digging this," I waved the smoke from my eyes. "I mean, no offense, but what if I told you that I don't want to get rid of Pete? What if I like having him and his spirit around?"

"*Awww,*" Pete cooed, misty-eyed, thumping his chest with his paw. "Right back at ya, daddy-o."

"Mister Keefe, don't you want your dog's spirit to be free to move onto the next level of the afterlife or wherever it is we all go after we die?" Sofi opined.

"Yeah, sure."

"Then I would inform you that your old dog isn't still hanging around because he wants to be here," Sofi continued. "It's because he feels he must stay out of loyalty. To you. Because you refuse to let him go."

"*Riiiiight,*" I guffawed at her outlandish statement. But then when I turned to see Pete's reaction, he went stone-faced. "Wait, is that true?"

"No. Not at all," Pete weakly shunned the idea.

"Pete, don't lie to me," I stared him down. He looked away uncomfortably, which he always did whenever he was hiding something. "Are you just sticking around here because you think I can't let you go?"

"*Well,*" he wavered, avoiding eye contact, "the thought did cross my mind."

I bristled, as Donny and Alissa fixed their eyes on me. I never thought of myself as overly fragile or dependent on my dog for my psychological well-being, but didn't want to appear vulnerable in such a communal forum. So, I turned it back on Pete.

"That's kind of hypocritical, don't you think?" I called out the little man. "I was grieving alone on my own for a good three, four months before you showed up. I didn't come to you. You came to me!"

"Easy, pops," Pete downplayed it. "I think you're overreacting—"

"No, I'm not overreacting. Just keeping it real," I ranted. "I even adopted a new dog, and started dating again before you came back to screw things up."

"Screw things up?" Pete denounced, while Donny, Alissa, and Sofi observed our exchange like spectators at a one-sided tennis match. "I *made* you. Do you honestly think you could've gotten this far if it wasn't for me—personally or professionally? I got you more phone numbers than you could shake a stick at. I wasn't just a wingman, I was your chick magnet!"

"I didn't need you to get girls," I sulked.

"Oh, really? You must be getting Alzheimer's then, because from what I remember, you couldn't even talk to a girl before I came along," Pete recalled.

"Okay, maybe I was a little shy."

"You were a nerd! An art geek. Then later after you became successful, you used me to get out of things, like, '*Oh, sorry, can't make it. I have to go home and walk my dog.*' There's a doggie door. I could help myself out, thank you very much."

"That is so like you. Taking all the credit," I seethed.

"It's not like you're a walk in the park either, pal. I gave you the best years of my life."

"Yeah, then you died on me!"

"Is that what this is about?" Pete bounced off the couch, hopping mad. "I didn't leave you—you left me! For *Gay Paree!*"

"And I'd do it again, too!" I yelped, as Donny, Alissa, and Sofi looked on, confused, but enthralled. "Because I have Brownie. This is my dog now," I snatched Brownie from Alissa's grasp. "And she's sweet and loving and a hell of a lot more affectionate than you ever were!"

Pete blinked at me crestfallen, the smart-aleck smirk wiped from his face. "Dude, are you serious? And I thought we were soul mates."

"No," I railed on spitefully, "you're not the dog I thought you were. You're a monster. A bully. Ever since you came back, you've been rude, crude, and selfish. Sarcastic. Disrespectful."

Pete teetered back in shock, as my below-the-belt insults battered his sheen of self-esteem. Even Brownie looked appalled, as her ears went back, and she buried her face into my forearm.

"Geez. Tell me how you really feel," Pete surrendered, his voice breaking, showing the most emotion I had ever seen out of him—dead or alive. And that's when I realized I might've gone too far. But in the heat of the moment, my pride wouldn't let me take back all the horrible things I said.

"I'll get out of here, so you and 'The Rebound Dog' can go back to your happy little lives," Pete said, and meekly turned and sauntered out of the room.

Then, as the smoke cleared from our big blowout, Brownie did something that she'd never done before: she bit me.

"Brownie—bad dog!" I set her down on the floor to punish her, but that's exactly what she wanted, as she sprinted off into the other room to go join her big brother in doggie solidarity.

"Fine, go take his side!" I shouted at the fluffy, little backstabber. "Traitor!"

I turned back to Donny, Alissa, and Sofi who were all sitting huddled together on the couch, wide eyed, and mystified at what they had just witnessed.

"Man's best friend?" I fumed. "Yeah, right. Bullshit."

"This is a first," Sofi uttered, putting away her sage. "After that, I think we all could use a drink."

Upset and incapable of entertaining company for another moment, I grabbed my jacket and stormed out of the house in a huff.

CHAPTER 13
DON'T SWEAT THE DOG STUFF

I walked all over town that night to do some serious soul-searching, however, my brain took a detour as I relived my run-in with Pete. Funny, if you would have passed by me on the street, you would've thought I was just out for a leisurely stroll—but inside I was raging like a maniac. I couldn't stop brooding about Pete's insinuation that I was the one who couldn't let *him* go. How dare that dog question my backbone? He was the one going around masquerading as a ghost, scaring the bejesus out of everyone!

As the blocks wore on though, my attitude softened. I tried to see things from Pete's point of view. He was dead right about one thing: I was inconsolable without the hairy curmudgeon. Even though I had cracked open my heart a little for Brownie and Janelle, I never felt strong enough to completely let Pete go and move on. I was still in love with my old dog.

In light of this breakthrough, it nearly got me killed, as I looked up to see a pair of high beams barreling straight for me in the pitch-black night.

The car screeched on its brakes, and time seemingly stood still, as the vehicle swerved across the road in my direction. Then there was a loud smash, and that was the last thing I remember. They say your life flashes before your eyes when you die, but all I saw was darkness.

When I finally came to, a glowing white light hovered over me, flickering luminously. Where was I—dead? In heaven? Or someplace else?

"Get up," a voice jarred me from my coma. "It's just a sprained ankle."

I swiveled my head to see Janelle sitting bedside with me in a crummy hospital emergency room, flooded with beeping monitors and flesh-dulling fluorescent lights.

"What happened?" I asked, confused to find myself swaddled in a baby blue paper gown and padded neck roll, hooked up to a maze of IV drip lines.

"You were hit by a car. But don't worry, you're going to be fine. You must have an angel looking out for you," she smiled serenely.

"Mmm, too bad I'm an atheist," I fidgeted with my bandages.

"Come on, I'll give you a lift home. It's the least I can do after almost running you over."

"Wait, you're the one who hit me?"

"It wasn't all my fault. You were walking down the middle of the street at night. If Milo hadn't seen you at the last second, we'd be planning your funeral right now."

"Milo—from the dog park?" I glanced out into the

hallway, and there was Milo, the tanned, heartthrob dog walker hunk, sporting a linen jacket and perfectly ripped jeans, flirting with two nurses.

"We were on a date," Janelle briefed me. "Our first date."

"I know him," I sat up, discomfited. Even though I was out of it, I still couldn't believe my ears. "Isn't he a little young for you?"

"Sounds like someone's threatened by my new young stud."

Janelle was right. This news was troubling. The way to this girl's heart was through dogs, and I couldn't compete with the younger, cooler, better looking Milo. Not to mention, he had the pedigree as a bona fide canine pro.

"But I thought he thought you weren't into dudes," I muttered, my words slurring from the drugs.

"What?" she looked at me cross-eyed.

"Never mind," I groaned.

"Okay, let's go, goofball," Janelle grabbed a wheelchair for me to ride in. "They need the room. They've got two knife victims out there bleeding all over the lobby."

If Pete could've seen me rolling across the hospital parking garage stuffed inside that oversized neck pad—my very own cone of shame—he would've laughed his ass off at the irony. We finally made it out to Janelle's ratty, old doggie van and I slumped into the back cabin chair, solidifying my role as her backup guy, while Milo took the front seat.

"Does it smell like dogs in here?" Janelle wondered aloud, as the suffocating dog scent blasted our nasal passages. "I've had this van so long I've forgotten what it smells like."

"It's a little ripe," I joked, even though I found the pungent odor strangely refreshing. "But if I was a Bloodhound, I'd feel right at home."

I glanced back at the pet crates stacked behind me, surprised to see no dogs there, just a bunch of tattered blankets and empty cages. "So where are all the kids? You didn't let them tag along for date night?"

"No, they didn't make it," she glanced over at Milo, visibly upset. "It was a really bad crash."

Oh, shit, I thought. Were some of her dogs injured during the car accident? I already had one dead dog on my conscience. I didn't need any more. Then she and Milo broke into hysterics, high-fiving each other, greatly amused by their inside joke.

"Gotcha!" Janelle buzzed. "Sorry, couldn't resist. I know how much you like that dark doggie humor."

"You should've seen your face," Milo added.

"Hilarious," I winced. "You guys make such a cute couple."

"Let the good times roll," Milo said, offering up a joint. "Anybody want to join me?"

"No thanks," Janelle politely refused.

"Yeah, me neither," I added. "I've got enough painkillers in me right now to drop a horse."

"Really? I thought for sure you'd be a stoner if you're hanging out with the ghost of your old dog," Milo crowed.

"You told him?" I glared at Janelle in the rearview, perturbed. "I'm glad my personal pain and suffering is comical to you two."

"Relax, it just came up."

"Yeah, we're dog people," Milo backed her. "There's no judgment here."

"Don't worry, we didn't waste that much time discussing you, Charlie," Janelle leered lasciviously. "We were too busy having sex."

I looked at her in disgust, and then she and Milo burst into laughter again. "Kidding! Do you really think we'd sleep with each other on the first date? Omigosh, the dog park would combust from all the gossip!"

We all chuckled at the ludicrous notion of her shacking up with the local dog walker stud. At least I was hoping it was inconceivable. Baked or not, the young buck, Milo, was more than up to the task, I'm sure.

"So here we are," Janelle pulled into my driveway to drop me off. "Goodnight, Charlie. Send my love to Brownie. And Pete, too, of course."

"I will," I slithered out the van's side door. "Thanks

again for the ride—and *not* killing me."

"Maybe we should've to put you out of your misery," Milo giggled, as he and Janelle yukked it up some more before driving off together, leaving me alone to make amends with my furry family members.

I turned and hobbled up the front steps of my darkened house. It looked spooky at night with all the lights off, and I was mad at myself for not leaving a TV or lamp on, which I had forgotten to do in my haste of stomping out earlier. I tried to wipe off the all-encompassing dog stink from Janelle's van, so Pete and Brownie wouldn't suspect I was cheating on them, as I limped inside, anxious to apologize for all of my transgressions.

"Pete, Brownie—I'm home!" I announced, turning on some lights to brighten the mood. Right away, I was surprised to find Brownie shivering on the couch all by her lonesome, looking terrified.

"Brownie girl?" I rushed over to put a blanket on her. "What are you doing out here all by yourself? Where's your big brother at to protect you from all the evil spirits?"

My goofy dog voice didn't appear to be very consoling, so I picked her up, and we went room to room looking for the big guy.

"Pete!" I called. "Where you at? Look, I'm sorry for going off on you tonight. That was way over the line. And I didn't mean all that stuff I said about you being rude and selfish. Okay, maybe the rude part," I blabbered, waiting for him to jump out behind some nook-and-cranny to scare the crap out of us at any moment. But he didn't.

"Where did he go?" I eyed Brownie for guidance. "Did he tell you where he went?"

She looked clueless, so we kept searching all over the house for Pete's whereabouts at his old favorite hangouts. In the bedroom. Under the bed. In the closet. Burrowed down inside the dirty clothes hamper. On the bathroom floor. Behind the dressers. In my studio. Below the tall bookshelf. The basement. The garage. The downstairs bathroom. The front porch steps. The back patio. His old dog house. Hiding inside the rolled-up tarp holder stashed underneath the deck. But he was nowhere to be found. My fast-talking, funny bone-tickling phantom had vanished into thin air.

Flustered, an eerie vibe settled over the house. Something felt different now than it had since Pete returned with his powerful presence. In fact, it felt just like that first night I had come home from Paris following his untimely death. It felt empty. Like my beloved old ghost of a dead dog had died all over again.

I grabbed Pete's plastic cone in the closet and used it as a bullhorn to call out louder for him. "*Peeee-eeeeete? Where are youuuuuuu?*" I yelled, my desperate pleas reverberating throughout the gloomy corridors, echoing off the walls, ceilings, and floors—only to be met with silence.

"*Peeeeete!* Where did you go-oooooooo?" I dropped to my knees, pleading over and over again, shaking the whole house with my ceaseless cries. "*Come back, Pete! PLEASE COME BAAAAACK!*"

CHAPTER 14

GONE DOGGIE GONE

Do you remember earlier when I said there was no quieter place than the home of a dog owner the day after their dog has died? Let me revise that. It's actually much, much quieter the day after your *talking* dog has departed. My house resembled a monastery without Pete's smart-ass wisecracks filling the dead air. Even Brownie was depressed from the sudden withdrawal of verbal taunts that she had become so accustomed to from the ghost formerly known as her big brother.

I replayed our fight over and over in my head, and wished I could've taken back all those hurtful things I'd vented out of anger. Honestly, the fallout stunned me because I didn't know that Pete—or this spirited form of him—was so thin-skinned. Sure, Pete was known to throw a tantrum if I stayed out too late or didn't feed him on time, but these flare-ups were always short-lived. This was a dog that thrived on spitting out one-liners like Don Rickles at a Friars Club Roast. Maybe Pete's stint in heaven had brought out his sensitive side. He could dish it out, but he couldn't take it.

Mostly, I was disappointed in myself for not better utilizing my extra time with Pete. I mean, how many dog owners had ever gotten the chance to speak with their deceased dog? This was a once-in-a-dog-time opportunity to explore the age-old questions concerning man and the meaning of life. And yet I had frittered away a large portion of that valuable time with him riffing on dick and fart jokes! This seemed highly irresponsible at best—and possibly even a crime against humanity.

So, I then decided to do what any other crazy, irrational dog lover would do if they lost their talking dog: I tried to get him back. I was willing to do anything I could to see Pete just one more time, so I enlisted a whole new psychic network of friends to conjure him back from the afterworld.

I dialed telepathics all over the globe—from California to Calcutta—to channel Pete. I traveled up and down the West Coast attending private séances with Native American medicine men and soothsayers. I posted help wanted ads on holistic healing blogs and forums seeking their prayers. I bought antique Ouija boards, and did tarot cards with Brownie. I put my money into the palm-reading hands of fortune-tellers who allegedly had a direct line to the other side, but that only made me more disconnected. I erected a mini-shrine of Pete outside The Carmel Mission and burned painted effigies in his memory. I put Pete's collar on around my neck and danced naked under a full moon, searching the stars for his face. I took blood oaths, secret pledges, and sacred vows in Pete's honor, but then when nothing happened, I took his name in vain. I even bought three new pairs of Nike running shoes and placed them all over the house in hopes that I'd find Pete's droppings in them by sunrise. Anything I could do to solicit Pete's spirit back from the hereafter, I did. And then some.

I know this sounds absurd, but I imagined if I could just build it, maybe, just maybe, Pete would come back again. Nonetheless, all of this mystical mayhem was to no avail, because after all the praying and positive energy and visualization techniques, the spiritual fireworks didn't cause one spark. Pete never showed his face.

Brownie was a good sport throughout these exercises—er, <u>exorcises</u>—but by the end, she grew tired of all the pomp and circumstance surrounding her long-lost brother. She just wanted to go back to her routine of three walks and two squares a day.

That said, I wasn't quite ready to give up on wooing Pete back just yet. I still had one more trick up my sleeve. I went back to the drawing board to do the only thing I really knew how to do in this world: paint. I may no longer have been able to see Pete or talk to him, but this was the next best thing to stay in touch.

I placed Pete's box of ashes on a mantel above my easel and got down to business. I didn't tell Donny what I was working on. I just worked. And it came pouring out of me. I locked myself in the studio and toiled away, putting in 16-hour days for weeks, taking only short breaks to feed Brownie and take her out to go potty. I'm not sure if it was divine intervention, but my juices were overflowing, as I quickly filled up several blank canvases with bewitching new renderings of Pete. When Donny called to check in that I was still alive, I told him there was no time for chitchat—I was busy painting—which I think both thrilled and unnerved him because he had become so conditioned to my consistent inconsistency.

Brownie, being the team player that she was, seemed spellbound by my productivity—although she wasn't too keen on getting splattered with paint whenever I flew into Jackson Pollock mode. Ideas and images were gushing out so effortlessly that my hands had a hard time keeping up. It was a mystery where this burst of creativity came from, but I wasn't about to question it. Maybe it was the indomitable spirit of Pete coursing through my veins, his saintly paw guiding my hand, pushing me to be a better artist, as I could hear his smoker's voice ringing in my head with every brushstroke, *"C'mon, man, is that all you got? You can do better than that."*

When the paint dried after my non-stop marathon, I took stock of what I'd done. The final tally was twenty-four oil paintings, seven watercolors, and a collage. Not to say quantity equals quality by any means, I was pleased to finally have something tangible to show Donny after having been so fruitless since Pete's exit.

As for the paintings themselves, I was surprised at what I saw since I couldn't remember sketching many of these pictures. Quite unlike my conventional happy doggie pics that I'd become known for in the last decade, these were strange, twisted, experimental puppies, shaded in ominous tones—ghost stories told in hieroglyphics—of Pete lost somewhere between life and death, Earth and space, heaven and hell.

They were my bleakest, yet in some ways most hopeful paintings about Pete's destiny. But would anybody else like them? It has always been difficult for me to analyze my own work. Generally, it's only after some time has gone by—months, even years—that I gain enough perspective for a true honest evaluation. If these creations didn't bring Pete back, then at the very least, they helped me illustrate my deepest, innermost thoughts about the next life and this bizarre out-of-body experience that we went through together.

Certainly, none of this hocus-pocus mattered to Donny because conveying deep, personal ideas didn't necessarily sell paintings—and often didn't. At the end of the day, this was business. And we needed to move inventory. During economic booms, when everyone is flush with spending money, it's easy to peddle pretty paintings to vacationing tourists. Conversely, during recessions, as the country was currently muddled in, our shop's finances can get dicey since nobody needs art to survive like they do food and shelter. It would be up to our customers to determine what, if any, monetary value these paintings had in the real world.

First things first though, I had to get my biggest supporter and harshest critic on board: Donny.

"Uhhh, yeah?" Donny answered, annoyed, when I called.

"Hey, get your big butt over here," I badgered him over the phone. "Gotta show you something."

"What?"

"What do you think? I told you I've been working my ass off. Got a bunch of new paintings for you."

"Okay, but can we do this tomorrow?" he yawned, hampering my enthusiasm.

"Why not now?" I asked. "You getting sloshed at a wine tasting?"

"No," he snorted, "it's two in the morning."

I looked over at the digital clock flashing on the microwave. *1:51 A.M.* I was so zoned out in my own trance that I had totally lost track of the time.

CHAPTER 15

THE SPIRIT OF SAINT PETE

"What the hell are these?" Donny cursed, as he barged into my studio the next morning to scrutinize the row of new paintings set up against the back wall. Still cranky from last night's wake-up call, this wasn't the response I was hoping for. Donny and I had reached the point in our art versus commerce relationship where candor took precedence. And he wasn't coy about sharing his opinions of my work.

"I take it you don't like them?" I lurched behind, losing confidence.

"It looks you were either dropping acid when you painted these—or the ghost of Salvador Dali is living vicariously through your paintbrush."

This clearly was not an endorsement. Salvador Dali, the legendary Surrealist artist from the 1930s, was renowned for his hallucinatory paintings of melting clocks dripping over desert landscapes—not joyful dog portraits.

"They're eye-catching," Donny resumed his critique, "but they're way too abstract with these flying angel dogs all over the place. The main problem is they just don't look like Charlie Keefes."

"Well, I think it's my most important work to date," I asserted. "And I'm sure Pete would agree."

"Oh god, don't tell me Pete painted these?"

"No, Pete's gone," I lamented. "He left."

"Again? Where did he go this time?"

"I don't know. But that's what inspired these paintings. So that maybe he would see them somehow and come back home. So I'm naming this series after him: *The Spirit of Saint Pete.*"

Donny looked dumbstruck. He didn't want to touch that with a ten-foot choke chain.

"So what are you trying to say with this work?" he turned back to the paintings. "That Pete's dead and gone forever?"

"No, what I'm saying is that Pete's life *here* may be over, but that doesn't mean he's not somewhere else. But these paintings aren't just about Pete. They're about anyone we've loved and lost. They practically painted themselves."

This wasn't some BS sales pitch. It's what I genuinely felt. Not that Donny was buying it.

"I can tell Brownie loves them," he skeptically pointed at Brownie snoring asleep in her dog bed.

"She's not a fan of pop art," I responded.

"Look, Charlie. I know you've worked really hard on these, but they're just not commercial."

"What? What does that even mean?" I flared up.

The term commercial has always infuriated me. And why did people who also had no inkling of what it meant always use it to back up their arguments? *Did you like the new Spielberg movie? "Nah, too commercial." Have you been to that Ethiopian restaurant? "It used to be good, but now the place is so commercial." How's your book coming along? "Awful. My publisher says the writing should be much less commercial."*

"These paintings are unsellable," Donny spelled it out for me.

"How do you know they're unsellable if you haven't even tried to sell them yet?" I fought back.

Concluding from our own sales history, there was zero demand for hippy-dippy dog paintings before we started selling them. The market found *us*.

"Because these paintings are just too dark for your audience," Donny said unequivocally.

"Edvard Munch's *The Scream* sold for a hundred and twenty million at auction—and that's dark."

"Yes, but Edvard Munch is a master of 20th Century Expressionism. You, no offense, are a Painter of Dogs."

"*The* Painter of Dogs," I corrected him. "And thanks for the ego boost."

"Charlie, when clients are paying thousands of dollars for a painting of yours to put up in their home, they want to see happy pictures of happy dogs that make them feel good and happy about life. Not be bummed out about their dead dogs rotting in hell."

"Maybe my art has evolved. People should explore deeper things. Like their own mortality. You need a little darkness to appreciate the light."

"People don't want to be lectured to," Donny prattled on. "The other risk is that by showing this super serious stuff, you could hurt your brand as an artist. If fans find out The Happy Dog Painter Dude is really deep down a dark, depressed, angry madman—they might not want to buy another one of your paintings again!"

He did have a point businesswise. But I was an artist, not a businessman—or a brand, perish the thought—so I threw all of this sound advice out the window.

"I hear ya, Donny, but have a little faith," I coaxed him. "Remember when I first showed up at your gallery fifteen years ago with my portfolio of dog paintings? You thought I was nuts."

"I still do," he shuddered.

"But then you took a chance. And look what happened. You sold a couple paintings that first week. Then three or four the next, and so on. We didn't know what we were doing back then, but here we are. Over ten years later. Still going strong."

"Not exactly strong," he counseled. "The landlord just notified me that we're still on the hook for three more years in case we try to break the gallery's lease."

"So, we've got nothing to lose," I pleaded my case. "You've got an empty gallery that needs a show—and I've got a studio full of brand spanking new dog paintings that need to be seen. Don't bet against Pete. He's gotten us this far. He'll get us over the next hump."

Donny turned and walked around the room to give it some thought, then stopped at a Chagall-styled painting of Pete floating through a starry night sky. He stared at it silently, intently for what seemed like an eternity.

"Okay, I'm in," Donny exhaled. "But this better work—or else we'll both be buried in debt."

I slapped Donny's hand, and we whooped and hollered with gusto. Brownie's head popped up, startled from her beauty rest by all the commotion.

"She's in, too," I smiled.

With this last-ditch Hail Mary, we could only pray that Pete was up there somewhere, looking down upon us with his blessing.

CHAPTER 16

THE ART OF THE DOG

Gearing up for this new show made me nostalgic for the good old days when Donny and I first embarked on our partnership. We pulled out the 'Let's Put On A Show' playbook to get the word out around town—handing out flyers, doing interviews with local newspapers, TV and radio stations—which isn't really that old school since most regional outlets publish links on their websites that can be accessed all over the globe. With all the art/culture/lifestyle blogs and social media events these days, every opening night is a world premiere. Still, it was invigorating to be taking a more pro-active approach, instead of just sitting back cashing royalty checks, while Donny handled the business end.

From the outside, it appears that most art gallery bashes just happen with little or no preparation. You send out the invites, hang a bunch of pictures on the wall, crack open the bubbly—and voilà, it's party time! *Au contraire*, my friend. For our little doggie art soirée, we needed pull out all the stops to garner some attention and make it a real happening, as my mom would say—for art collectors both here and abroad.

Keeping in line with the somber tone of my Saint Pete paintings, we transformed the showroom into an afterlife theme by installing dramatic track lighting, and painting the white walls black and blue to create a mysterious ambience, making the space look more like a haunted workshop than an art gallery. Regardless, I believed that the majority of people who RSVP'd had heard the rumors about my ghost dog sightings and just wanted to come see if Pete's portraits would start levitating off the walls. But we didn't care what the reason was that brought them—my art, or the prospect of paranormal activity. As long as they showed up, it was our duty to entertain them.

I went against my convictions by allowing Donny and Alissa to dress Brownie up in a pink sequined jacket and fake diamond-studded collar like she was a sexy starlet—as we stationed her inside to work the front door as our Official Host/Greeter/Smeller of Butts. Having spent so much time laying the groundwork for this shindig, Donny and I had high hopes going in. But our optimism wouldn't last long. How excited can you be when the first guest to show up is your own mother?

"Mom, you made it," I said, giving her a big hug, as she blew inside all gussied up in a billowy lavender blouse.

"Of course I made it. Pete was like a stepchild to me. We never talked, but we had an understanding." She looked around and realized nobody else had arrived yet. "Where's everybody at?"

"It's 6:30," I double-checked my watch, hiding my

nervousness. "We just opened."

"Reminds me of your birthday party in second grade," she turned to Donny, filling him in. "We just moved to town and invited Charlie's entire homeroom class, but nobody came. It was so sad. I went door to door knocking on all the neighbor kids' houses to—"

"Mom, please don't," I rolled my eyes. "I'll start having flashbacks."

"Okay, I know you're busy," she kissed me on the cheek, as a line of new guests shuttled in past her. "You get back to work. I'm going to enjoy the show." She twirled around and came face to face with a morbid painting of Pete resting in a coffin. "*Oh dearrrr.*"

Worrying about offending Mom was the least of my troubles though because then the dogs showed up—literally—as to make it a real pet-friendly affair, we encouraged our guests to bring along their own four-legged pals to add some fun and frivolity to the evening. (Unfortunately, all cats were left off the guest list for security purposes.)

In hindsight, our pro-dog policy turned out to be a huge blunder as my artwork on display was not the most suitable exhibit for canine audiences. I should've known the subject matter might be too daunting. Nobody wants to be told that his or her dog will die someday, especially the dog. It was like forcing toddlers to sit through an R-rated slasher flick. The dogs' faces—and their owners—were bright and chipper upon entering the otherworldly venue, but then after viewing my Pete-In-The-Afterlife paintings, they quickly turned glum. Although dogs are commonly assumed to be colorblind, judging from their adverse expressions to my work, they appeared to pick up every minute detail.

At first I thought it was a technical glitch that was causing all the stunned, deer-caught-in-the headlights responses. Could our guests not clearly see the dark paintings set against the murky black and blue walls? However, these fears were soon dispelled once we overheard the ugly boos, hisses, and audible gasps that blasted our senses in passing. And those were just the dogs! The humans were not as kind as they could not be so easily bribed with water and bully sticks. You know you're in trouble when your partygoers would rather skip the free booze and just leave than be subjected to your art for another second.

Tonight was supposed to be a new beginning by laying out my bare naked soul—and Pete's—for all the world to see. But after the first twenty minutes, it was clear that our dead dog art extravaganza was turning into an old-fashioned horror story. No two ways about it. These dog lovers despised my dog paintings. And the crushing part was that these were fans that actually *liked* my work, and had bought items in the past. These were friends and family, carefully cultivated clients and collectors, who were cherry-picked just for this special occasion. If they didn't like my new stuff, no one would.

Like most artists, I tend to internalize rejection, so these people not only hated my Pete pictures—they were saying, in effect, that they also hated me.

I caught Donny's eye across the crowded room and his doleful look said it all. We were D.O.A. His initial instincts were proving to be correct. Historically, during big dog and pony shows like this, we typically had already sold a dozen or so pieces to special preview members before the show had even opened. But tonight we weren't getting a nibble. Nothing. Nada. Not even a single inquiry about prices or availability, or even a courtesy request to skim the catalog.

Bless Donny's heart though. If he knew the ship was going down, he didn't throw me overboard. He just kept working the room, refilling glasses, mixing in with the dejected dog owners and their dogs, trying to keep everyone upbeat—or at least not plunging into the abyss.

And then to add insult to injury, Janelle showed up. With a date. Milo. They barely set foot in the door before Brownie leapt up to smother her with kisses, happy to see a familiar face—and whiff a yummy scent—among this hot, jumbled mess of strangers.

"Brownie! How's my lil' cutie pie?" Janelle bent down to pet her costume-clad body. "What are you wearing—Versace?"

"Thanks for coming," I plastered on a feckless smile

to greet her. "You're just in time to watch my career go up in smoke."

"Wow, this place looks dead," she glanced at the dismal faces scattered about the room. "Did the ghost of Pete scare everyone away?"

"No, but he better show up soon. We need all the help we can get," I turned to shake hands with her handsome dog walker date. "Milo, how you doing?"

"Heyyyyy," Milo's bloodshot eyes gaped at the paintings, already stoned. "These are fucking rad, bro. I thought you were just a wannabe artist. You're the real deal."

"The jury's still out on that," I shrugged.

Milo was even more galvanized when he saw the waiters serving free drinks. "Is this thing open bar?"

"Yeah, help yourself," I obliged.

"*Sweeeeeet*," he playfully nudged Janelle. "What do you want, babe? On me."

"Whatever you're having is fine."

As soon as Milo left, I smugly turned to Janelle. "You guys look happy. Can't even tell the age difference."

"Believe it or not, we actually have many things in common."

"Like what—you're both of legal drinking age?"

"No, mostly just a deep love for sushi rolls and blow jobs," she shot back to rankle me.

"Good for you. Hope it lasts. Watch out for these

young whippersnappers though. They get bored fast. You just haven't seen his dark side yet."

"No, he's pretty much shown me *all* his sides," she joked with a toothy grin. "He's very comfortable in his own skin."

"Touché," I smiled through gritted teeth.

"So these are your new ones?" Janelle turned back to my paintings filling the room. "My, you've been a busy boy."

"Yup per."

Feigning appreciation, she took an extra long pause to study a charcoal portrait of Pete getting sucked down a black hole. "They're very...neat."

"Neat?" I cringed at the backhanded compliment. "You don't have to say you like them just because I did them. They're not for everyone."

"Or *anyone*," she added, noting the sullen spectators nearby. "I'm teasing! You know I love anything with dogs in it—but I do enjoy it more when the dogs are still alive."

Janelle's reason was valid since she had dedicated her life to saving dogs from impending doom. I had to give her that much.

"Dude, these pictures are *sooooo* trippy!" Milo blared, as he strutted back to join us double-fisting two cocktails. "I love how you weave the heaven and hell narrative together. Good versus evil. God versus the devil."

I nodded in agreement, as Milo articulated some more insightful interpretations that he had drawn from my work. It was quite surprising coming from him, as I wrongly assumed that he was a guy only interested in black light posters of Led Zeppelin and The Grateful Dead. Frankly, I had no clue what he was talking about, but it was nice to finally hear something positive.

"You know," I confided to Milo, "these paintings were partly influenced by you."

"Really?"

"Yeah, well, something you once said," I recalled. "Right around when Pete died, you told me about the two types of dog widowers."

Milo squinted, baffled by my story.

"Don't you remember at the dog park?" I continued. "You said there are two kinds of dog widowers. Those that go out and get a new dog right away, and those that grieve for their old dog for the rest of their lives."

"I said that?" Milo looked flummoxed, but pleased with his own astuteness. "Shit, bra. That's intense."

Donny then came over to say hello. He had a big smile on his face, but I could tell something was amiss. "Janelle, you look stunning. As always."

"Thank you, Donald," she acquiesced. "You're the only person I know who can wear a cashmere sweater to a dog show and not get a single dog hair on you."

"Mind if I steal Charlie for a sec?" Donny pulled

me aside urgently, not waiting for a response. "We're in deep shit."

"What? We ran out of alcohol?" I asked.

"No, out of interest. All the big buyers took off. And this party's dying faster than your dead dog pictures on the wall," he fretted. "We still have two hours to go."

"So what are you hearing? Any early reviews?"

"Not good. I just got six Tweets in a row from a blogger called ArtFiend. There's blood in the water. We're getting crucified."

"Big deal," I said. "It's just one blogger. The art world's filled with hateful bloggers."

"Yes, but this one has 250,000 followers, and he just uploaded this," he held up his iPhone to show me an Instagram pic of a pooch taking a huge dump on our gallery floor, accompanied by the caption, *DOG ~~ART~~ FART*, as one of my Pete paintings hung drably in the background.

This is why I've never been good with constructive criticism—since most criticism today on the Internet is not all that constructive. The naysayer's aim is purely to harm, showing off their witty daggers, in order to draw attention to themselves.

"Where is this punk?" I looked for the culprit. "I'll crap all over his Twitter feed."

"Don't bother, he's gone. Alissa already cleaned up the mess."

"You were right, Donny," I let out a heavy sigh. "I should've listened to you. These paintings are unsellable."

"Hang in there, we're not giving up yet," Donny straightened his tie, resolved to turn this night around. "But we're going to have to do something quick before this party really goes down the toilet."

CHAPTER 17
HOW MUCH IS THAT DOGGIE
(PAINTING) IN THE WINDOW?

Donny hopped up on a stack of apple boxes in the center of the gallery showroom, eagerly tapping his wine glass to get everyone's attention.

"Ladies and gentlemen, please don't leave," he broadcast to the meandering crowd. "We're just getting started here! This is a party. *Wooo-hooooo!*" he lampooned. "First of all, thank you. Thank you so much for coming out tonight. Charlie and I cannot tell you how much we appreciate you all being here with us this evening."

"Woof-woof!" someone jeered, eliciting a few awkward titters.

"Now for the important announcement," Donny said, pulling out his bag of tricks. "Charlie and I are going to do something that we've never done at an opening before. Ever. We're going to have a live auction tonight. So this is your chance to own a Charlie Keefe original—signed personally by 'The Picasso of Pooch Portraits' himself!"

The subdued audience politely clapped, as Donny's wife, Alissa, yanked a framed Pete portrait off the wall, and paraded it around the room for theatrical effect.

"All right, first up on the block is *Pete and the Holy*

Ghost—a God-fearing dog meets DaVinci composition. And we will start the bidding at one thousand dollars," Donny presented. "Don't be frightened, ladies and gentleman. This is a bargain."

Indeed, it was a risky move to offer the painting so far below market price, but we had to get the ball rolling. Yet, as Donny looked out into the throng for takers, a lackluster mood permeated the room. It got so quiet so fast that you could've heard a silent dog whistle.

"Yes, that's right," Donny bolstered his proposal. "This is a Charlie Keefe original. Signed and dated by the artist. And yes, I am starting the bidding at one thousand dollars—not *ten thousand*, which is customarily what Charlie's paintings go for. Do I hear a thousand?"

Silence. If this show was to honor Pete, no one in the crowd was reaching for their wallets to pay tribute. Standing against the back wall watching this epic failure unfold with Mom, I noticed her hand shoot upward to bid.

"Don't, Mother," I tackled her against the stucco partition, horrified, pinning her arm down to her side.

"What?" she resisted. "I'm trying to help."

"That's not helping!"

"Going once, going twice..." Donny offered one last time. No sale. "Okay then, how about we select another painting? Say, something more uplifting?"

Alissa seized another picture—this one, a slightly rosier depiction of Pete sitting on a bed of heavenly clouds behind a prison fence of pearly gates. It wasn't what you'd call a cheery portrayal since Pete's essence was imprisoned, but the blue skies and fluffy clouds in the backdrop belied a sunnier outlook.

"This one's called *Pete At The Pearly Gates*," Donny indicated, as a few buyers stepped in for a closer look. "And we will start the bidding at five hundred dollars. Do I hear five hundred?"

Again, no one pounced. Even the dogs were mum. My greatest fear was now unspooling before my very eyes. In my heart, I felt this series of paintings was the best, most important work that I had ever done—but now the marketplace was telling me something entirely different.

"Did I tell you all how much Charlie and I really, really, *really* appreciate you for being here tonight?" Donny implored, scoring some laughs. "Okay, and did I also mention that we will be donating a percentage of the proceeds from tonight's auction to our good friends at Foster Dogs Forever?" he waved to Janelle for confirmation. "Isn't that right, Janelle?"

"Sure, fine by me," Janelle gave him the thumbs-up.

"There you have it, folks! Who has five hundred bones for a pup painting and a donation to a really great cause? Come on, it's for the dogs!"

Tragically, even this bonus offer—a work of art,

plus a dog charity write-off for Pete's sake—did nothing to aid our venture. There were no bidders.

This is it, I thought. The end of the road. I tried to console myself with the fact that Van Gogh only sold one painting during his lifetime. I should consider myself lucky. I had a good run. And now my luck had simply run out. They say every dog has its day—and by the looks of it, Pete and I's best days were coming to a swift, humbling end.

"*Whoooo*, tough crowd," Donny hiccuped, searching for something to sweeten the pot. "All righty, because Charlie and I are feeling extra generous, we will lower the opening bid to two hundred and fifty dollars. Whaddaya say? Do I hear two-fifty? This is such a steal—we should be arrested. You can't even get a reproduction for that!"

Still nothing. Donny scanned the room for a confidant, or someone with deep pockets, anything to keep hope alive, if not an art fan, at least a pro-dog advocate. He met eyes with Helen Galloway, a wealthy socialite, known for her houseful of Yorkies and charitable endowment of the local arts. "Mrs. Galloway, not to put you on the spot here, but can you do two-fifty for some abandoned puppies?"

"No thanks," the elegant patron demurred. "Not my cup of tea."

Where had all the magic gone? I marveled. Less than six months ago, Donny and I had dog art aficionados lining up to buy my paintings, begging us to take their money just to be given an opportunity to be put on a wait-list. Now the roles were reversed. I was still the same artist painting the same dog, except now that lovely dog was dead. The stench of Pete's death had spooked all the buyers away.

"Do I hear two-fifty...*please?*" Donny stared out futilely into the audience, his voice trailing off. "Going once, going twice—"

Then finally, and mercifully, someone yelled out, "Two-fifty!"

This would be me. I couldn't stand watching any more of this catastrophe, so I brashly strode up to the front of the room pumping my fist in victory.

"Um, you're going to purchase your own painting?" Donny looked at me incredulously.

"Hell yeah, I love it. Gonna sell it for ten times that on Ebay," I vowed.

"Oh, come now, folks. Let's not make Charlie buy his own work. Let's help him out, shall we?"

"No, they had their chance!" I waved him off. The crowd had turned their backs on me, so being the mature, responsible adult that I was, I turned on them.

"Box 'em up, I'll take 'em all," I said, grabbing my Pete pictures off the walls. Milo and Janelle tried to pull me back to save my dignity, but there was no going back now. The damage had been done.

"Easy there, tiger," Donny reprimanded me. "Don't

be a drama queen."

"This is my boy, Pete!" I cried out. "Don't you get it? God, I miss him so much," I bent over to smooch Pete's oily face on one of the paintings. "This dog had more heart and soul in his little ghost body than all you heartless souls have in all your bodies combined!"

In retrospect, it was inappropriate of me to take out all my anger and frustration on this genteel congregation, but that's just how it went down. I must've scared the living daylights out of half the people there—and I only say half—because the other half had already left since I launched into my diatribe. My outburst not only inflamed the guests, it fired up the dogs as well, as they started yipping and yapping uncontrollably.

"Okay, auction's over," Donny informed the crowd, his voice drowned out by the rising doggie chaos. "Thanks again for coming. G'night!" Then he woefully turned to me. "Charlie, I think you better go home, too."

"Okay, but I'm taking these with me," I pouted, stacking up the best of my Pete pieces to haul away. "Damn, these are heavy. Maybe I'll just take a few and come back later for the rest."

I readjusted my grip, but then tripped over a Maltese standing behind me and she yelped feistily, which provoked the other dogs to snap at one another. Pretty soon, it was pooch pandemonium with several more mutts breaking free from their owners, scratching and clawing up the walls, knocking over paintings and sculptures, turning the place into a doggie cage match.

Demoralized, I spun around hopelessly to see a Siberian Husky sink his teeth into one of my pious Pete paintings and a Bull Mastiff tugged viciously on the other end, playing tug-of-war with the sturdy canvas until it ripped apart, spitting out chunks of Pete all over the place.

"No, stop it! *Nooooooooooo!!!*" I squealed, as the primal hounds stampeded past me out the doors. "That's my boy—*that's my boyyyyyyyyyyy!*"

CHAPTER 18
WANTED DEAD OR ALIVE

After the doggie brouhaha was over, it looked like a tornado had swept through the gallery. The pristine walls were splattered with muddy paw marks, gashes, saliva stains, and dog knows what else. A third of my collection was ruined. Donny, Alissa, Janelle, Milo, and Mom and I just stood there in defeat.

"Your father would've been so proud," Mom commented, breaking the silence.

"Right," I crumpled. "Thanks, Ma."

"No, seriously," she said with all sincerity. "Dad really loved dogs."

"No, he didn't," I contested.

"Where in the world did you get that idea?"

"He *murdered* Starsky. The dog wasn't even sick— and he put him down."

"Excuse me?" Mom reared up defensively. "That dog had a tumor the size of a grapefruit. I was there. Starsky was in such terrible pain. It nearly killed your father to do it. I'd never seen him cry about anything before until he put that darn dog to sleep. That's why we never got another dog. He couldn't go through losing another one."

"Really?" I sputtered, ambushed by my mother's

bombshell disclosure. All that time I'd wasted doubting my deadbeat dog killer dad was now wiped clean. In a way, I felt vindicated knowing that even my tough-as-nails father had shed a few tears over his dog dying.

"How come you never told me that before?" I asked Mom.

"You were nine. Your father didn't want you kids to see him crying over a stupid dog. Men were different back then," she covered her mouth to yawn. "Okay, time to go home. Need a ride, honey?"

"No thanks, I'll walk," I started to leave, and then stopped, realizing that I had forgotten my most important belonging. "Wait, where's my baby?"

"Don't worry, your paintings will be fine here," Donny assured me. "We couldn't give these away."

"No, I meant Brownie," I kneeled down to look under the tables and chairs. "She was right here a second ago."

Soon, everyone joined me in searching for Brownie amid the party debris of used plastic cups and paper plates.

"Brownie?" I called out. "Brownie!"

If you thought I was distraught about not selling the Pete paintings, you should've seen the look on my face when I realized that Brownie was missing. Nothing will put things more in perspective than losing your puppy. This sweet dog had never left my side since I'd taken her in—and then she pulled off this vanishing act. It was so out of character.

Had Brownie grown tired standing around all night hearing stories about her ex-big brother, the gruesome ghost of honor, and left in a hissy fit? Or maybe she'd gotten trampled during the mass exodus? Being the affable, earnest host that she was, perhaps she had thought it was her duty to personally walk each guest home. I had placed her by the front door during the show thinking it was a safe refuge from the heavy foot traffic, but it only ended up providing her an easy getaway.

"Has anybody here seen my dog?" I raced outside to catch the last wave of stragglers milling about the sidewalk. "She's a little brown and white King Charles Cavalier."

"Yeah, she just flew off with Casper the Ghost," a cruel bystander cackled.

Enraged, I bull rushed the guy, ready to rumble— but Janelle stepped in between us, "Look! Isn't that Brownie's jacket?"

She hurried over to pick up Brownie's itsy-bitsy, pink sequined doggie jacket lying balled up by the gutter, orphaned.

"You made your dog wear that?" Milo jabbed. "Looks like a stripper's outfit."

I frantically leafed through the jacket, finding her sparkly zirconia collar and dog tags still attached. I'd seen the little escape artist pawing at the cumbersome getup all night trying to get it off. This compounded my concerns because that meant even if somebody did find Brownie, she was no longer sporting any identification.

This set off more sirens. Did she get clipped by a car and take off scampering into the countryside? Maybe she tried running away back to her old Sacramento stomping grounds? *What a lousy dog owner I was!* How could I be so self-absorbed and wrapped up with my dead dog—that I neglected the welfare of my living one? Maybe tonight Brownie had looked up at all those metaphysical Pete paintings and saw the writing on the wall: this man's heart was not big enough for two dogs and never would be. Like a new girlfriend sick of hearing about her beau's ex, she took off to go find a better life for herself.

"Hey," a teenage girl walked up, "I think I saw your dog."

"Where?"

"There was a brown and white one playing with two bigger dogs out here. Then this rich-looking guy and his kids just drove up in a ginormous Range Rover and put them in back and drove away. I figured they were all his dogs."

"Oh my god," Janelle exclaimed. "The Fosters!"

"What?"

"The Fosters who fostered Brownie before. We drove past them on the way here tonight. They must've seen Brownie outside the gallery and stole her back!"

"What should we do?" I turned panic-stricken. "Call the police?"

"No, I'm sure it's a misunderstanding," Janelle tried to calm me down. "They're probably just ticked off at me since I told them Brownie was dead. Let me call them." She pulled out her phone to dial The Fosters, but then hung up, discouraged. "Voicemail."

"Let's go to their house and get her back," I demanded.

"Which one?" she scoffed. "The Fosters have two homes. One in Pebble and another smaller mansion down past the Highlands."

"Why do they have two houses so close to each other?"

"Because they can," she said.

We entered the south entrance of the 17-Mile Drive and wended our way up the scenic route until we arrived at a security checkpoint for the Fosters' gated neighborhood, which was only a stone's throw from the prestigious Pebble Beach golf resort. A private uniformed guard suspiciously approached Janelle's dog mobile with the garish logo on the side.

"Hi, we're here to see the Fosters," Janelle volunteered, as we all smiled nervously, on our best behavior.

"Are they expecting you?" the guard checked his watch. It was after ten p.m.

"No, but it's very important," she added. "It's about a dog."

The guard nodded warily, and went back inside his booth to make a call.

"This place is insane," Milo peeped ahead through the tall trees, where you could make out the palatial rooftops of the multi-million dollar estates tucked away from public view. "Is it paradise or a prison?"

"The Fosters are not available," the guard brusquely returned. "I'm going to have to ask you to leave."

"No, they stole my dog," I protested. "And we're here to get her back!"

"Sir, please leave immediately or I will call the authorities."

"That's okay, we'll try again in the morning," Janelle politely waved, and drove off, to my dismay.

"What are you doing?" I quarreled. "They've got my little Brownie fudge cake in there!"

"Relax, Charlie. I have a plan."

Five minutes later, Janelle pulled into a hidden dirt pathway down the road and parked her dog mobile, shutting off the lights.

"If they're not going to let us in the front door," she declared, "we'll just have to go in the back."

We all got out and started to hoof it through the pitch-dark forest *Mission Impossible*-style, as we heard the residents' dogs barking in the distance. As our feet crunched over the thick underbrush, I looked down and realized that we were hiking over a minefield of broken twigs and lost golf balls, the hazards of living next to a golf course. Milo lit up a joint.

"Put that out," I admonished him. "They'll see us!"

"Who?" Milo refused. "The only things out here are owls and raccoons. Besides, I can't be out in nature without smoking a bowl."

"So this is what you find appealing?" I turned to Janelle. "No wonder your romance life stinks."

"Yeah, I know, because all the great guys living with the ghosts of their dead dogs were already taken," she joked, then stopped to a halt. "*Shhhh!*"

"What?"

"You hear that?" she lingered.

We ducked down behind a fallen redwood tree, and through the clearing, we could see directly into the luxuriously landscaped backyard of the Fosters' grandiose home, where their two German Shepherds were stalking the grounds. The manicured lawn was so lush, green, and spacious that you could've mistaken it for a PGA fairway.

"There they are," Milo puffed, as the picture-perfect Foster family was loading luggage into a Range Rover, obviously getting ready to travel somewhere.

"There's Brownie!" I pointed at my girl being chased around the swimming pool by the two tween-aged kids. "Those brats better not throw her in the pool—she doesn't know how to swim!" I stressed. "Where are they going this late anyway? You think they're trying to go on the lam with Brownie?"

"Anything's possible with these people," Janelle bleated.

"Now we just have to get past those German Shepherds," Milo took another hit.

"Oh, that's Tyson and Dempsey," Janelle crooned. "I fostered them for a month. Total sweethearts."

Just then, the Shepherds heard us scheming and promptly charged in our direction, crawling up the fence, snarling ferociously.

"Unless they re-trained them as attack dogs," Janelle reconsidered.

Suddenly, a torrent of alarms sounded, piercing the night, as a bank of floodlights switched on to illuminate the backyard like a Major League Baseball stadium.

"*Run!*" Janelle screamed, and we took off sprinting back the way we came, slipping and sliding over the wild jungle of golf balls, rolling our ankles with every step. We did not make it out of the trees before we were surrounded by a squadron of security guards on golf carts, sticking flashlights and Taser guns in our faces.

"Freeze, this is private property!" a guard called out. "You are trespassing."

Janelle, Milo, and I were taken in and detained at the Pebble Beach Security station to answer questions and fill out crime reports.

"Here," one of the guards handed Janelle the phone. "Mrs. Foster would like a word with you."

"Hello?" Janelle answered apprehensively.

"Janelle, Elizabeth Foster. I see that you called me nine times in the last hour. Ever heard of texting?"

"Sorry, I wanted to catch you in person. It's about Brownie—"

"Oh, we know all about Brownie. Or we thought we did," Mrs. Foster curtly responded. "Imagine our surprise tonight when we saw Brownie had come back from the dead—alive and well, out on the town. How could you lie to us after all we've done for you and your rescue group?"

"I'm sorry I lied to you," Janelle looked over at me, "but I was looking out for the dog first. And in this case, I just felt the other owner's home was a better fit for Brownie."

"A better fit than *us?*" Mrs. Foster's snobbish voice crackled over the speakerphone. "I highly doubt that. That dog won the lottery when we picked him."

"*Her,*" Janelle remarked.

"Excuse me?"

"Brownie's a girl dog, not a boy dog."

"Whatever, I don't have time for this nonsense. We're on our way to the airport right now to catch a red-eye to New Zealand—"

"So where's Brownie? Is she with you?"

"Funny you should ask," Mrs. Foster said sharply. "We planned on taking her along on this trip, but then you and your friends intruded on our property, which activated the security gates and Brownie escaped."

"What? Did you find her?"

"No, but that's not our problem—"

"What do you mean it's not your problem?"

"If you hadn't trespassed, the gates wouldn't have opened for her to get away!"

"So you just left for your flight while Brownie's running around lost in the woods somewhere?" Janelle chewed her out. "What's wrong with you people?"

"Sorry, it's out of our hands now," Mrs. Foster sniveled. "Goodbye. Oh, yes, and don't count on any more donations from our family."

Click. She hung up.

Upon hearing this latest development, I felt even worse than I did when we learned that Brownie had been kidnapped. At least when she was taken hostage by the Fosters, she was under their care— however careless they might have been. But now Brownie was out there all alone. At night. In the dark. She could be anywhere.

After Pebble Beach Security released us with a $384 ticket for trespassing, the clock struck midnight. But Janelle was just getting to work. Using her dog rescue maestro superpowers, she called up all her contacts who were still awake at this hour—and put out the Bat-Signal, an all-points bulletin, assigning us into search teams to fan out all over the Monterey Peninsula area to cover different parts of town.

The Brownie hunt was on. We looked high and low for my girl, combing every charming little side street and country road in hopes of tracking her down. Donny and Alissa went around downtown Carmel replacing our expired art show flyers with *LOST DOG:* $$$ *REWARD* $$$ posters.

On my way to the dog park, I passed by several police cars and other locals on the lookout. Even two of the Pebble Beach security guards who had taken us into custody helped out with the expedition. It was heartening to see so many complete strangers—most of whom never had the pleasure of meeting Brownie— taking time out of their busy lives to assist in mine, but I guess dogs do bring out the best in people.

Despite that, as the night wore on with no new information coming in, my positive feelings soon turned negative. It was impossible to tell if we were on the right trail to locating Brownie, or just barking up the wrong trees.

I texted Janelle to see if she had any updates on Brownie. Two seconds later, my phone rang.

"Sorry, Charlie, nothing yet," Janelle said ruefully. "We're calling off the search for tonight, but don't give up hope. If Brownie's still out there, we'll find her. And if she turns up at any of the county shelters, they'll see the microchip."

"What microchip?" I asked.

"It's a chip we insert into all of our foster dogs in case of things like this."

"So, it's like a tracking device?"

"No, it doesn't have GPS. It's for ID purposes only."

"Then what's the point?"

"Charlie, I run a dog rescue, not a parole office," she said. "Just get some sleep. We'll get back at it first thing tomorrow."

CHAPTER 19
GHOST OF A CHANCE

I staggered back to my empty shell of a house and went to bed. Or should I say, I tried to go bed, but my brain wouldn't shut off, and kept whirring with wicked scenarios of Brownie churning in my head. What if she got nabbed by some dog-fighting gangbangers out cruising for fresh meat to feed their trained killers? Or what if she'd been attacked by a pack of coyotes and was bleeding on the side of a road somewhere? I could not stop visualizing her ambling down some dark, dead end street, or shivering under a clump of thorny bushes trying to stay warm. Contrary to the unknown mystery of her past life, Brownie had demonstrated to me that she was definitely *not* an outdoor dog. She was 100% lap dog, as her soft, cuddly physique was ill-suited to deal with any prolonged exposure to the wet, windy cold.

I prayed for her safe return, but even God probably cringed upon hearing my pitiful pleas:

Oh, God, please please help me find my dog, Brownie...I mean, I know you're kinda busy. Who gives a crap about a lost dog, right? But I love her so much. I'll do whatever you want—because I know this is a HUGE favor to ask. And I know I'm not very religious and haven't been to church in a VERY, VERY LONG TIME, so I don't deserve you doing me any favors, but if you could make an exception just this once...I'll make it up to you, I promise! I love you dear God, oh please please pleeeeaaasssssseee!

I never know how to end prayers, so I just whispered goodnight and laid there. Waiting for a miracle to happen. But nothing happened. I reached over and grabbed my cellphone on the bed stand to see if there was any missed any calls from Janelle. *No New Messages.*

After another fitful hour of tossing and turning, I closed my eyes and finally drifted off to sleep, but then was awakened by a noise from the other room. I thought it was nothing, and then heard it again. I got up and lumbered out to the living room to investigate. I stepped outside to see if the gusty winds had blown a tree down or tipped over the trash cans, but there was nothing out of the ordinary.

Then I heard the sound again coming from the kitchen and went back to check it out—and, to my delight, there was my Brownie girl standing outside in the moonlight, pawing at the side door to let her in. I rushed over to rip open the door, "Brownie! Where were you? I've been looking all over for you! Thank god you're okay!"

She jumped into my arms licking me like a spaz, and then gazed soulfully into my eyes, as she blurted out, "Sorry, dude, it's just a dream."

POOF!

My eyes fluttered open, and I realized I was still in bed. My visions of Brownie were only wishful thinking. The clock said *4:37 a.m.* I knew I wasn't going to get any more rest, so I got up for real this time.

I shuffled into the kitchen to make some coffee, and noticed the 40-year-old bottle of tawny port from Donny shimmering in the glass cabinet above. There was still a tiny bit left. Was it too early to have a drink, or too late? Screw it. I dumped a shot into my coffee and took a healthy gulp.

"Dang, pops. Hittin' the sauce already?" I heard a voice grumble behind me, and I whipped around—and there was Pete, the ghost of my ex-dog aglow by the fridge. "You're not going to find Brownie in the bottom of that cup."

"Pete?" I stammered unsurely. "Is that really you or am I dreaming again?"

"Nope, it's me," Pete answered.

"You're back!" I roared, throwing my arms around him. "Oh, I missed you so much. I'm so sorry for yelling at you and being such a—"

"It's okay. It's over. Don't drool on me," he pushed me away, shaking the slobber off his fur.

I wanted to say something profound to capture the moment, but I couldn't think of anything, so I just stared at him, mesmerized. "You're back," I repeated. "I knew you'd come back!"

"Whoa there, not so fast, daddy-o," Pete cautioned. "We gotta go."

"Go where? You just got here."

"We gotta find Brownie," Pete reminded me. "I didn't come back just for you. I came for my little sister. And to say goodbye. For good this time."

My head sank, disappointed.

"Hey, stop feeling sorry for yourself," Pete coached. "We've got work to do."

"Good luck. The whole town was out all night looking for Brownie, but nobody has seen hide nor hair of her. Not even a blip from her microchip."

"Microchips are overrated. I've got something better than that—ghost dog sense. I can see, smell, and hear things you people can only dream about."

"You know where she is?"

"I have an idea. Let's go, get your shoes on. Time's a wastin'."

I jumped up excitedly and raced over to put on my Nikes--but then felt a thick, cool, squishy substance envelop my foot. Ghost dog poop.

"*Haaaahhh!*" Pete cracked up laughing at his old prank. "I can't believe you fell for that again."

After scrubbing my toes clean, Pete and I piled into the car and set off to find Brownie before sun up. The bone-chilling fog had spilled in overnight, along with my rising dread. Lord only knew how much longer our girl could survive in these unpleasant conditions.

"So how'd you know that Brownie went missing?" I asked Pete.

"I don't want to be a name-dropper, but I got a call from one of the higher-ups. Not the big D-O-G though."

"You mean G-O-D?"

Pete turned hush. He wasn't talking.

"So is that where you went after you left us again—back to dog heaven?" I prodded him.

"I toldja, man. Can't talk about it," Pete stared at the road ahead, poker-faced.

"Come on, I won't tell anybody. It'll be our secret."

"You know how lucky we are they even let me come back a second time?" Pete preached. "They don't do this for just anybody, you know."

"Okay, you don't have to tell me everything. Just the high points."

"No," Pete stonewalled, "I can't give you the answers."

"Why not?"

"Because that would be cheating. Trust me, this thing's much bigger than us. So just shut up and don't ask me any more questions 'cuz you're putting my immortality in danger here with all this loose chatter."

I let it go and we headed south down Highway 1 toward Big Sur to continue our Brownie search and recovery mission, but we didn't come across any new clues on the trail. And the frustration was mounting, as the Pacific Ocean's waves pummeled the rocks below.

"I thought you said you knew where she was," I hounded Pete.

"Hey, just because I'm a ghost doesn't mean I'm psychic. We'll find her. You gotta believe," Pete said. "Okay, take a left here."

I turned left, and we drove a quarter-mile to the next intersection. "Take another left," he ordered, so I took another left. Then we hit a stop sign at the end of the road. "Left," he regurgitated.

"That's four lefts in a row—we're going in a circle!" I yelled. "All that time up in heaven has messed up your dog sense."

"Sorry, I've never been good with directions."

"This is crazy. We'll never find Brownie in a million years going like this! And she's out there somewhere, freezing, scared to death."

"She ain't scared," Pete frowned. "She's just pissed."

"Pissed at who?" I asked.

"You," Pete said.

"Why would she be pissed at me? She knows how much I love her."

"Well, speaking as her big brother, who's also a dog—"

"*Was* a dog."

"Whatever, let's just say I know her in a way that you don't. She got sick of playing second fiddle and you taking her for granted. Even girl dogs need to feel appreciated sometimes. Must be rough growing up in the shadow of so much awesomeness," Pete bragged. "But I'm partially to blame here, too."

"Huh?" I flinched. "What are you talking about?"

"I shouldn't have come back so soon right after you got her," Pete revealed. "But I got a little jealous when I saw how much fun you were having with your new dog. I didn't want you to forget me."

"Forget you? How could I? I was a mess after you died. Where were you the last four months when I couldn't get out of bed?"

"I know, guess I just missed all the attention. I missed *us*. Don't get me wrong, heaven beats the crap outta this dump, but I really love ya. And I'm sorry I never showed you before. So that's why I'm tellin' ya right now," Pete said, dabbing the corners of his eyes with his paw, trying hard not to break down crying.

"Awww, dude, I love you, too," I said.

Pete looked away to avoid eye contact, so he wouldn't start bawling, "Sheesh, stop it. Now you're really gonna make me cry."

I laughed.

"What?" Pete whimpered. "I may be a ghost, but I'm still human, y'know." I gave him a look. "You know what I mean."

"I know, buddy," I told him. "You're a big, macho, tough guy, but it's okay to express your emotions every once in a while."

"Stop—"

"No, it's nothing to be ashamed of. I know this isn't easy for you, but it really means a lot to me—"

"No, I mean *stop*—the car! *STOPPPPPPPPPP!!!*"

I glanced up to see that we were speeding right for a billboard sign with the *FOSTER DOGS FOREVER* logo on it—and then spotted Brownie hunkered down in front of it. She popped her head up, the whites of her eyes bulging back at us, petrified. All I remember is trouncing on the brakes, and Pete and I looking at each other helplessly, our faces frozen in terror, as we skidded side to side across the gravel road in slow-motion, screaming for our lives.

After the dust settled—which could've been seconds or hours, it was all a blur—I felt a dog's tongue licking my nostrils, and looked up to see Pete floating over me.

"Dang, what you trying to do—kill me again?" he griped.

I coughed, groggy, blinking through my swollen eyelids to make out Pete's angelic figure backlit by the sunrise on the horizon. "Am I dead?"

"Nah, you ain't dead. Just lucky," Pete said. "That air bag saved your butt."

I looked around, dazed, and saw the extensive damage done to my Toyota, as the front end was embedded into the FOSTER DOGS FOREVER sign like a cartoon missile. The windshield was cracked down the center in a spider's web pattern with smoke rolling out of the grill. The steering wheel hung sideways off the panel. Auto parts were scattered on the floorboards amid the loose change and wrappers.

Outside up ahead, the lights in Janelle's house snapped on. I could see her peering out at me through an upstairs window, wondering who or what the hell had just torpedoed through her front wall. Then I heard a shrill, high-pitched dog whine coming from under the car. Brownie.

"Oh my god, Brownie? Where is she?" I turned to Pete, but he just looked away, prying himself off the dashboard. "Oh, no, did I hit her? No!"

I rammed open the driver's door with my shoulder and fell out of the car to see my poor, sweet Brownie lying behind the rear left tire, her body heaving up and down, gasping for breath.

"Brownie?" I cried, crawling over the rocks like a brave soldier risking his life to save a fallen comrade. "*Nooooo-OOOOOOOOOO!*"

"Dude, chillax," Pete barked, hopping out to join us. "She's not dead—she just had a long night. She's sleeping it off."

Suddenly, Brownie's cute, little muffin head sprung

up and she bounded over and tackled me backwards
into the grassy knoll, showering me with kisses, as if we
hadn't seen each other in years.

"Brownie, you're alive!" I shrieked. "I love you so
much. Yes, I do—yes, I do!"

"Geez, why don't you two get a room?" Pete
heckled.

"Sorry, don't mean to rub it in your face, but I
thought for sure she was a goner."

"She ain't the brightest bulb," Pete grunted. "What
kind of dog sleeps outside in the middle of the road?"

"Charlie? *Char-lieeeec!*" Janelle bustled up to the
accident scene in her terry-cloth bathrobe with a flock
of foster dogs nipping at her heels. "Omigosh, you
found Brownie! Where was she?"

"Right here in your front yard," I said, embracing
her. "She must've gotten homesick. Or just sick of my
cooking."

My totaled car then broke off the gated wall's
hinges and crashed to the ground, a scrunched slab of
rubber and steel.

"Sorry about your sign," I shrugged. "I'll paint you
a new one."

"You're like a magnet for car accidents," Janelle
ribbed me. "It's a miracle you survived that."

"Yeah, well, Pete said it was the air bag that saved
me."

"What air bag?" Janelle took a gander into my

passenger window to survey the destruction. "This car doesn't have an air bag."

I went over to see for myself that there was no air bag deployed, nothing. And then it hit me. It wasn't the air bag—it was Pete. He was my miracle. I turned around to thank him, but he was already walking away up the hillside.

"Pete!" I yelled after him. "Hey, you lied to me. The air bag didn't save me—*you* did."

He just smiled. "So what, you callin' me a liar? I've been called a lot worse than that before."

"Wait, where you going?"

"Catch ya later, daddy-o," he smirked, climbing the hill. "I'm late. Got a hot date with Lassie."

"C'mon, don't go yet," I pleaded with Pete, as he marched past a line of foster dogs respectfully making way for him, giving him the full 21-dog salute. "I need you—*we* need you! This family's big enough for two dogs!"

The fuzzy little silhouette of Pete stopped at the top of the hill and turned around, lifting his right paw to wave one last goodbye. And then he did something that I'd never seen or heard him do before in all of our years together: he let out a long, mournful, beautiful howl.

"Goodbye, Pete," I waved my arms wildly. "*Goodbye! Thank you for being such a great dog! I love you—I'll NEVER FORGET YOUUUUU!*"

And then just like that, my dear old ghost of a dead dog did a couple victory circles and disappeared over the hill. And I knew right then and there that he wasn't coming back. It was time for me to let him go and move onto the next adventure in that great big dog park in the sky.

"Charlie?" Janelle interceded. "Who are you yelling at? Is Pete here?"

"Uh, no, he's gone," I said. "But we'll see him again someday, won't we, girl?" I rubbed Brownie's tummy, her silky-smooth coat was wet and tangled, soaking with gunk from her big night on the town. "Young lady, how did you get so filthy? Where were you all night?"

I looked down at Brownie's face and could tell by the twinkle in her eye that she must have had one amazing story to tell. Thank goodness she couldn't talk though, or else we'd be up all night again.

"That's it, you're grounded," I teased her with my goofy, amped-up dog voice. "You're never leaving home again!"

"Um, Charlie, just a word of advice," Janelle noted. "Don't ever talk to your dog like that in front of women. It's not a turn-on."

We laughed, and then she kissed Brownie on the forehead. "Sweetie, you must be starving. Let's go get you something to eat."

We turned and started walking up the long country lane toward Janelle's farmhouse, and she slipped her hand into mine. "I'm glad you're okay," Janelle told me. "You must have a mighty angel on your side."

"Yeah, but I think he prefers to be called Messenger of Dog," I quipped, and then noticed the lights still on inside her house. "So, where's your boyfriend, Milo? He didn't spend the night?"

"No, the dogs kicked him out," she said. "If my dogs don't like you, you don't stand a chance. Plus I think he was paranoid that they were going to eat all his weed."

KISS HIM GOODBYE

A few days later, I decided it was time to spread Pete's ashes and free him forever from his paltry wood box. Janelle, Brownie, and I took Pete up to his favorite spot in the park where he used to love to dig, but then I couldn't settle on just *one* favorite spot to disperse Pete because just about everywhere I went reminded me of him. So, I guess you could say that a little bit of Pete went a long ways that day, as we sprinkled handfuls of him all over town.

"Here we go, Pete, this is it," I released the last of his ashes into the breeze. "I don't know where you went, but I hope you're in a better place. And if you want to show us any signs to let us know you're okay, that would be cool, too."

We all bowed our heads in silence, waiting for something magical to happen, but nothing did—except Janelle's cellphone started ringing. And it wouldn't stop.

"You mind?" I said pointedly. "How 'bout a little respect?"

"It's not mine," Janelle held up her phone to show me. I checked my phone, and it read: *DONALD BERGMAN CALLING.*

"Shoot, it's me." I sheepishly answered, "Hello?"

"Charlie, how we doing?" Donny's peppy voice greeted me on the other end.

"How do you think I'm doing? We're at Pete's funeral," I said. "Thanks for coming by the way."

"Sorry, some of us have to work," Donny replied. "Call me when you're finished up with the services."

"No, go ahead. Party's over," I tossed Pete's empty, old Ikea box into a nearby recycling bin. "What's up?"

"You're not going to believe this, but I just got off the phone with London. Do you know who Lady Eva Kepler is?"

"No."

"She's a distant relative of the British Royal family and also happens to be a major art collector. And apparently her 22-year-old Jack Russell terrier just died."

"And so? Is that supposed to cheer me up?" I asked.

"No, but a friend of hers showed her your Saint Pete paintings online—and she absolutely loved them and wants to buy some."

"Which ones?"

"All the heaven ones you still have left," Donny snickered. "Can you believe it? Isn't that fantastic?"

"What about the ones in hell?" I asked. "They go together, they're a set."

"Sorry. She only likes to look at the bright side."

I wobbled, taken aback. Even though nobody else

cared for my last portraits of Pete, I had grown attached to them in all their unappreciated splendor. Part of me was happy that they hadn't sold so that I could keep them all for myself.

"So what do you say, Charlie?" Donny asked. "You there? What do you want to do?"

I gazed up into the sky overhead and could've sworn I saw Pete's face form in the cottony clouds—and then dissolve. I'm not sure if this phone call was a sign, but whatever it was, it would help get our gallery out of the doghouse for the time being. And it was so like Pete. Even in death, he was still helping my career.

"Sounds good," I told Donny. "Let's do it. We'll drop by later to help ship them out."

Brownie sidled up beside me proudly wagging her tail. She didn't say it, but I could tell that she was okay with taking one more day out to honor the memory of her big brother. No doubt Pete would've wanted it that way.

It has been almost a year now since Pete's death. And putting my talking ghost dog to rest has brought some much-needed closure, but it has also raised more questions. I still really have no idea where he went off to. Whether he's hanging out at The Rainbow Bridge, partying it up with Lassie, Old Yeller, and Spuds MacKenzie, or if he's been vaporized in the universe somewhere and has forgotten all about his past life down here with us. I just hope that wherever he is that he's happy and enjoying himself. I hope that doggie heaven is even greater than he says it was—although he never did really give me all the facts on that for sure.

And even though Brownie's more than enough dog for me now, I look back fondly on that extra time Pete and I had together, and I thank my lucky stars. Time is a funny thing. The more days that go by since I last saw Pete, the more I feel him slipping farther and farther away. And part of me questions if he ever really existed in the first place. I sometimes think to myself, right after I tuck Brownie in goodnight and before I fall asleep, maybe I was crazy. Maybe none of this was real. Maybe I just dreamed up this whole crazy ghost dog episode as some kind of weird, post-pet traumatic stress disorder. After all, no matter how much I loved Pete, he was only just a dog. Just a dog! Just a rude, crude, goofy, grumpy, irrepressible, irresistible, lovable dang dog.

But then I smile because deep down I know the truth. He wasn't just a dog. He was *my* dog. I may not be able to see him, smell him, touch him, hear him, or talk to him anymore like I used to, but I know he's still there. Watching over me. And he always will be.

Oh yeah, and as far as my relationship with Janelle is concerned, I called her to have dinner next week. And not just a doggie play date. A real date. We'll see how it goes. I've done the two dog thing; let's just hope that I'm man enough to handle two females in my life.

In Memory of

Petey Ryan (1996-2010)

&

Charlie Dickens (2011-2013)

ACKNOWLEDGMENTS

Big, happy dog licks to my wife, Sandy, whose patience, good humor, and editing skills were invaluable in the completion of this novel. Likewise, my true blue friend, Tommy Nohilly, also deserves a hearty scratch on the belly for his many helpful suggestions and dirty dog jokes. And, of course, how could I write a book without thanking my lovely parents, Michael and Shirley Ryan, who have been so supportive all these (dog) years—and bear absolutely NO resemblance whatsoever to the guilt-producing parents featured in this book. Love you, guys!

A special thanks also to Bernadette Peters for her unique insights and, more importantly, for all the wonderful work she does at Broadway Barks, the annual star-studded pet adoption event in New York City. Additional thanks goes out to Patty Saccente, as well as Edie Jarolim at WillMyDogHateMe.com, for taking a peek at an early excerpt with her keen editor's eye.

In conclusion, I would like to mention the countless dog owners, dog walkers, and dog friends that my wife and I have met in San Francisco and Los Angeles over the years, including Andrew and Caroline Kaps (& Johnnie & Gabby), Richard and Susan Glasson and their stud Border Collie, Champ; Wild

Bill Peacock, Richard Harris-Deans (Gigi & Momiko), Morgan Tubman, Pat Schone and Chris Reed (& Bella & Lulu & Jasmine), Steve and Sharone Karsh (& Lola), Craig Maddux (& McKinley), Maureen (& Brueggel), Stacy Earl (& Muggsy), Johanna Chandler (& Cody), Michael Kircher, and the late "Dogwalker" Jim Pollack, to name just a few. Their precious dog tales from Crissy Field all the way down to Santa Monica's Ocean Avenue are still ringing in my ears.

Last but not least, I cannot go without mentioning our family's beloved Jack Russell terrier named Petey, a proud boy who introduced us to the wonderful world of dogs. It has been a while since he left us back in 2010 at the age of 14-and-a-half, but it feels like only yesterday.

Sad to say, our rebound dog, Charlie, a happy-go-lucky Terrier-Retriever mix, also died suddenly after eating a poisonous mushroom right before publication. We miss him terribly, but are truly grateful for the short time that we had together.

Being a dog widower has taught me that it doesn't matter if you have a dog ten years or ten months—the pain and hurt is still the same. Fortunately, the good part is that the love never dies!

*A portion of the sales of this book will be donated to Muttville Senior Dog Rescue in San Francisco, CA.
http://www.muttville.org

ABOUT THE AUTHOR

RUSS RYAN has written and developed screenplays with several Hollywood producers, including the makers of *American Pie*, *Final Destination*, and *Fireflies in the Garden*, and has a writing credit on a really bad teen comedy, National Lampoon's *Repli-Kate*, starring Eugene Levy. This is his first novel.

He is also the creator of Meansheets.com, a vintage movie poster blog that focuses on the greatest artists and illustrators from the 1940s-1980s.

For more information about *It's Just A Dog* and to satisfy all of your dog book cravings, please go to the official website/blog at:

http://www.ItsJustADogBook.com

Email Russ Ryan: **ItsJustADogBook@gmail.com**

Connect on GoodReads
http://www.goodreads.com/itsjustadog

Like on Facebook
http://www.facebook.com/itsjustadog

Follow on Twitter @itsjustadog:
http://www.twitter.com/itsjustadog

Did you enjoy this dog book or is it for the dogs?

Please leave your thoughts with an
honest review (none too good or bad — haha):

http://www.amazon.com